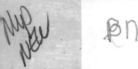

βMc

Murder Carries a Torch

MURDER

Carries a Torch

A Southern Sisters Mystery

Anne George

WHEELER
PUBLISHING, INC.
ROCKLAND, MA

★ AN AMERICAN COMPANY ★

Published in Large Print by arrangement with William Morrow, a division
of HarperCollins Publishers Inc., in the United States and Canada

Wheeler Large Print Book Series.

Set in 16 pt Plantin.

Library of Congress Cataloging-in-Publication Data

George, Anne.
   Murder carries a torch: a Southern sisters mystery / Anne George.
      p. (large print) cm.(Wheeler large print book series)
   ISBN 1-58724-127-7 (softcover)
   1. Patricia Anne (Fictitious character)—Fiction. 2. Mary Alice
(Fictitious character)—Fiction. 3. Women detectives—Fiction.
4. Sisters—Fiction. 5. Alabama—Fiction. 6. Large type books. I. Title.
II. Series

[PS3557.E469 M85   2001]
813'.54—dc21   2001047441
                                                               CIP

To Irene Hendricks and Jake Reiss,
the best friends that any writer could ever have.

Chapter One

"I'm telling you, Patricia Anne. Fred kissing the ground like he did was a little too much. Embarrassing."

"He slipped."

"Slipped, my foot. The man was on his hands and knees patting the concrete, saying, 'Thank God.' It's a wonder everybody didn't fall over him."

I glanced around at my sister, Mary Alice, who was standing at my utility room door watching me put clothes in the washing machine. She had on a gray pants suit with a cream-colored turtleneck sweater and had already informed me that she was on her way to a luncheon.

I was one of the ones who had nearly fallen over my husband Fred at the airport, but I still felt the need to defend him.

"He hates to fly."

"Well, I figured that out for myself about an hour out of Birmingham. Every time I spoke to him he growled. Did you hear those

1

noises? Pure growls. And he didn't even chew the peanuts. He trashed them." Mary Alice chomped her teeth together. "Like that. Thank God I wasn't sitting next to him on the Concorde. You've earned your place in heaven living with that man for forty years." She paused. "Why are you spraying Windex around that shirt-sleeve cuff?"

"Because I haven't had a chance to go to the store. This works as good as Spray 'n Wash." I put the shirt into the machine, closed the lid, and turned on the warm cycle.

"How come you're not jet-lagged like I am?" I asked. "I feel like there's a weight on top of my head."

Mary Alice moved from the doorway and I followed her into the kitchen and collapsed onto a chair.

"I have more reserves than you do. More stored-up energy. You want some coffee?"

I nodded that I did. She got two mugs, poured the coffee, and pushed the sugar toward me.

"You see," she explained seriously, "it's simple. I'm slightly larger than you, and that little extra fat gives me more energy. If you would eat normally, you wouldn't be so tired."

Little extra fat. Slightly larger. Ha. The woman is six-feet tall and weighs two hundred fifty pounds. Admits to that. No telling what she really weighs. Especially after hitting every good restaurant in Warsaw, Poland, where we had been for the last two weeks spending Christmas with my newly married daughter Haley. And, believe me, there are some good restaurants there.

"You probably lost weight in Warsaw," she continued.

"I may have. All that walking."

"And not eating."

I poured milk into my coffee and watched it swirl around. No way I was going to get into this argument. Mary Alice has never believed that it's genetics that made me a foot shorter than she is and a size six petite. She swears it's lack of nutrition.

"I had an E-mail from Haley this morning," I said. "She's missing us."

"Well, of course she is. Nobody speaks English in Warsaw. Nobody. And there's not even so much as a Wal-Mart. Just all those museums, old as the hills, and you have to ride those rickety streetcars to get anywhere, for heaven's sake."

"I thought it was a beautiful city."

"Well, you see, that's the difference in you and me, Mouse. I like things to move a little faster."

"You mean like interstates?"

"And better TV. Their *Wheel of Fortune* was pitiful."

I sighed and let Mary Alice ramble on. Haley was very happy, and she and her new husband, Dr. Philip Nachman, considered it the opportunity of a lifetime to be spending the first few months of their married life in richly cultured Warsaw.

"I'll say this, though." Mary Alice took a sip of her coffee. "Nephew seems to be making Haley happy."

The "nephew" bit is going to take a little

3

clarification. Mary Alice's second husband was also Philip Nachman. Haley's new husband is his nephew, named for his uncle. So Haley and Philip are Mary Alice's niece and nephew (Philip by marriage). The "nephew" is to keep from confusing him with the original Philip Nachman, dead and buried at Elmwood Cemetery beside Sister's other husbands long ago, but still alive (so she says) in her heart. Certainly in her bank account. Each of her three husbands left her richer than the preceding one.

She leaned forward. "Don't you think so?"

"What? That Haley's happy? Sure."

"It's the Nachman genes." She stirred her coffee. "I almost asked Haley, but I decided not to."

"Asked her what?"

"Well, my Philip, when we were making love, just before he'd," Sister paused. "Well, he had this unusual thing he'd do."

"What?"

"He'd stop for a second and say, 'Lord, the saints are marching in.' " She smiled.

I thought about this disclosure for a moment. "Somehow I don't think that's genetic, Sister."

"Probably not. He did go to Tulane. But every time I hear that song I get misty-eyed. I wanted to have a New Orleans band play it at his funeral, strutting down the path at Elmwood with their umbrellas, but I wasn't sure it was kosher."

"I wouldn't think so."

Mary Alice looked into her coffee cup thoughtfully. "He was a lovely man, Mouse.

Very much in touch with his inner child. No big alpha male hang-up like Fred has."

"Alpha males don't kiss the ground when they get home."

"Ha. I knew he didn't trip." Mary Alice got up, put her mug into the dishwasher, and turned to face me. "I might as well tell you, Mouse. I've made a New Year's resolution to get married this year."

"To Cedric?"

"Who?"

"The last man you were engaged to."

"Of course not. I'm serious." She leaned over the counter toward the table where I was still collapsed. "I was thinking while we were crossing the Atlantic that my 'sell by' date is fast approaching and I want some steady company, preferably someone who can dip me when we dance."

"Just keep changing your 'sell by' date. That's what *20/20* says they do at all the grocery stores. You've already backed it up two years." On her last birthday, Mary Alice had been sixty-six, but had decided to count backward from now on. I am now three years younger than she is instead of five.

"Oh, I plan to. I still think it's time I settled down, though."

"Bill Adams?"

"I don't know. Maybe. He's a little alpha."

What was this "alpha" stuff?

"Fairchild Weatherby?"

Sister straightened up. "No way. Terrible things happen to his wives, like people murdering them."

"Is age a factor here at all?"

"Of course. Forty to eighty."

"Well, that narrows it down. I'll be on the lookout."

"I'm serious."

"So am I."

I watched her get her purse and put on lipstick. "What kind of luncheon are you going to?"

"An Angel Sighting Society lunch at the club."

"Well, have a good time."

"I will."

As soon as the back door closed, I went into the den, lay down on the sofa, and pulled the afghan over me. As I was sinking into deep sleep, the question flitted through my mind, an angel-sighting luncheon?

Muffin, Haley's cat, woke me up about an hour later kneading the afghan and purring. I rubbed between her ears, and she stretched out beside me.

"Your mama sent her love," I told her. "She'll be home in a couple of months."

Muffin purred louder.

"We saw our first-ever white Christmas."

Muffin drooled.

"Your grandpapa says one is enough." I snuggled deeper under the afghan and smiled, thinking of Fred struggling through Warsaw's snow, swearing that we had all lost our minds, that he had seen on CNN that it was sixty-five degrees in Birmingham. He had enjoyed seeing Haley, though, enjoyed seeing how happy she was with Philip. And Fred was back at his beloved Metal Fab today, jet-lagged, but at home. And probably a little disappointed that the metal-fabricating industry had survived for two weeks without him.

I was trying to decide whether to go back to sleep or get up and put the clothes in the dryer when the phone rang.

"Did I wake you up, Aunt Pat? You sound sleepy."

"No, hon. Muffin did that about two minutes ago. How are you feeling?"

Debbie, Mary Alice's middle child, the outcome (as I had just learned) of the march of one of the elder Philip Nachman's saints, is eight months pregnant. Having been there three times myself, I knew my question was dumb.

"Better than I felt with Fay and May at this stage. Remember how I had to have help getting up out of a chair?"

Debbie's twins, Fay and May, are almost three. Not interested in marriage, but very interested in motherhood, she had opted for the UAB sperm bank. Then, last year, she had met Henry Lamont and married him with a speed that surprised us all. Now she was expecting David Anthony Lamont in a month.

"I remember." I pushed the afghan back and sat up. Muffin jumped down disapprovingly and headed for the kitchen.

"Well, when I talked to you yesterday, I forgot to tell you that Pukey Lukey has been trying for several days to get hold of you or Mama. When he kept getting your answering machine, he called me and asked where you were."

Luke Nelson is our cousin who lives in Columbus, Mississippi. He is a very nice man who was unfortunate enough to suffer from monumental car sickness when we were children. Mary Alice says Luke's bouts were volcanic eruptions. His mother was our father's only sibling, though, and he adored her. So a trip to the beach frequently meant holding towels like shields.

"He didn't leave any messages," I told Debbie.

"Well, you might want to call him. I asked him if there was something I could help him with, and he said no, that he needed to talk to one of you. He really sounded worried."

"I wonder what about."

"Don't have any idea."

"I'll call him." I paused. "By the way, Debbie, do you know anything about an angel-sighting society?"

"A what?"

"An angel-sighting society. Your mama said she was going to an angel-sighting society luncheon at the club."

"No, that's a new one. Did Mama sight some angels in Warsaw?"

"She mainly shopped. Fussed about everybody speaking Polish."

"I hope our diplomatic relations are still intact."

"She did enough shopping to assure that."

"Good. Well, I've got to get to court, Aunt Pat. You wouldn't believe how easy it is to win a case when you're eight months pregnant."

"Give Fay and May a kiss for me, and give

David a pat." I hung up, smiling. It was still strange to me to know that much about an unborn child. And nice.

Muffin was taking a bath on the kitchen table. I looked out of the window and saw my old Woofer dog asleep in the sun in front of his igloo doghouse. I put the clothes in the dryer, fixed a peanut butter and banana sandwich, poured a glass of milk, and settled down to watch *Jeopardy!* All was right with the world. I even knew the answer to the Final Jeopardy question.

I'll blame it on jet lag. I had every intention of calling Luke as soon as I quit talking to Debbie. Instead, after *Jeopardy!* was over, I made out a grocery list and went to the Piggly Wiggly. Usually, this time of year, I have all kinds of leftovers from Christmas and New Year's in the freezer. This year, thanks to Warsaw, the cupboard was bare. The night before, our next-door neighbor, Mitzi Phizer, had brought us over some chicken Tetrazzini and salad. Fortunately. We were even out of Lean Cuisines. Mitzi had taken care of the animals for us while we were gone, and she brought each of them treats, too. They were so glad to see her, it hurt my feelings. Woofer actually whined when she went through the gate on her way home.

After I got home with the groceries, I still didn't remember to call Luke. I made a meatloaf, peeled some potatoes, and took Woofer for a short walk. Birmingham is no Warsaw, climatewise, but it's still pretty chilly on late January afternoons. A couple of blocks, and

Woofer and I were both ready to call it a day. He had reestablished his territory on every tree, and I was cold.

While I was taking the clothes from the dryer, though, I remembered. I found Luke's number on the list I keep in the end-table drawer and dialed it. No answer. No answering machine. I looked at my watch. Almost five. His wife, Virginia, was probably out somewhere and had forgotten to turn the machine on. And Luke might still be at his office.

I dialed the office number. No answer. No answering machine. Slightly strange, but nothing to worry about. I finished folding and putting up the clothes while I enjoyed the good smells of a January meatloaf wafting from the oven.

Half an hour later, I dialed both numbers again. Still no answer. I called Mary Alice to find out if Luke had left a message with her. I also wanted to know more about the angel sightings.

"Nope," she said. "Why? Is something wrong with him?"

I told her what Debbie had said.

"He probably just wants us to do some politicking for Richard, which I'm not about to do. He has too many teeth and he always looks like he's just blow-dried his hair."

Richard, Luke and Virginia's son, is a second-term member of the House of Representatives so not everybody agrees with Sister.

"This isn't an election year. Besides, this is January."

"Oh, Mouse, you dummy. It's *always* election year."

"I guess you're right. How was your luncheon?"

"Interesting. Two women sighted angels while we were in Warsaw."

"Where did they see them?"

"One woman said she woke up and the angel was standing by her bed."

"Writing in a book of gold?"

"What?"

"Like Abou Ben Adhem."

"Who's he?"

"Never mind. What about the other one?'

"She was having a root canal done."

"How did she know it was an angel?"

"She just knew. We had a good lunch. Not chicken, thank goodness. I had enough of that in Warsaw. Broiled salmon in dill sauce."

"That's nice. How did you get invited?"

"Half the investment club's in it, Mouse. All you have to do is believe in angels."

"And you do."

"Of course. Don't you?"

"Maybe."

"I think that would get you in. Look, if you talk to Pukey, don't promise him a thing about politicking."

The back door opened and Fred walked in.

"Gotta go," I said. "And I won't." I hung up.

"Meatloaf." Fred held his hand to his heart. "I could just cry."

So much for the alpha male.

"Are you tired?"

"Beat. Everything's in pretty good shape over at the shop, though." He came over and hugged me. "You know what I'm going to do? Take a shower and put on that new jogging suit Haley gave me for Christmas."

"Be still my heart. I'll light a fire and we'll watch *Wheel of Fortune*."

Which is what we did. By eight o'clock, both of us were sound asleep, Fred in his recliner, me on the sofa. Around twelve I woke up enough to turn off the gas logs and the TV and get us both to bed. It was the next morning before I remembered Pukey Lukey and tried to call him again. It was the next morning when there was still no answer, that I began to worry something might be wrong.

Chapter Two

E-MAIL
FROM: HALEY
TO: MAMA AND PAPA
SUBJECT: MISSING YOU

We're missing you so much, but wasn't it a wonderful Christmas. We had three new inches of snow last night. Papa, you'd love that. Have you talked to Alan and Freddie since you got home? I E-mailed both of them right after you left and haven't heard a word. Tell them to do better toward their sister. We're invited to a party at the university tonight in honor of some visiting professor who everyone thinks will win the Nobel Prize in chemistry. I've never heard of him, but Philip is real excited. Tell Aunt Sister I'll wear the blue outfit she gave me for Christmas. Is everything okay at home? How's the jet lag? Debbie says David Anthony is getting huge. I wish I could see her.

    I love you.

E-MAIL
FROM: **MAMA**
TO: **HALEY**
SUBJECT: **EVERYTHING'S FINE**

Thanks again, darling, for the wonderful Christmas. The jet lag is better today. Aunt Sister says I have it worse because I don't have her physical reserves. She went to an Angel-Sighting Society luncheon yesterday at the club. Two members claimed they had sighted angels recently. I've talked to both Alan and Freddie since we got home. They both had good holidays. E-mail them again and fuss at them. Haven't seen Debbie yet, but I remember her with Fay and May. I never thought she would look normal again, let alone get her figure back, which she did.

    Do you believe in angels?

    I love you.

When I turned off the computer, I realized I was hungry, really hungry for the first time since we had gotten home. I put three slices of bacon in the microwave, scrambled a couple of eggs, and fixed some cinnamon toast. Comfort food. I sat at the kitchen table with the January sun coming through the bay window and ate every bite except for a small bit of egg that I gave to Muffin. So much for the anorexia that Sister claims I have.

I was having my second cup of coffee when I remembered Luke and reached for the phone. There was still no answer at either number. I dialed Mary Alice.

"Maybe they've gone skiing," she said.

"Skiing? Have you lost your mind? They're both in their sixties and have lived in Mississippi all their lives."

"You don't have to ski to go skiing. You sit in the lodge and drink hot rum and watch the ambulances go by."

"You can do that in the bar of the Holiday Inn across from University Hospital."

"Not the same ambiance. Everybody wouldn't have on the pretty ski outfits."

"Well, I doubt seriously that Luke and Virginia are sitting in a ski lodge drinking hot rum and watching ambulances."

"I don't know why not. At Debbie's wedding they were both crocked."

"I'm hanging up," I said.

"Wait. You know that red velvet bag I gave you to put in your purse when we came through customs? The one I told you to guard?"

"The one with your pearls in it?"

14

"Yes. That one. I'll be over in a little while to get it. Guard it."

"I'll get Fred's old BB gun out. How come you didn't get it yesterday if it's so precious?"

"I forgot it."

This time I did hang up. I put on a pair of jeans, a turtleneck, and an old flannel shirt of Fred's and took Woofer for his walk. As we opened the gate, I could see Mitzi Phizer sitting in her new sunroom reading the paper. She and her husband, Arthur, our longtime neighbors, had gone through some terrible problems back in the fall. It was good to see her there; it was good to see her wave at us.

The air was so crisp you could taste it. Warsaw, in spite of the cold and snow, had had the underlying smell of diesel fumes and coal fires. Fred was right. It was good that home was this particularly beautiful place.

We turned the corner and I could see the statue of Vulcan, the huge iron god of the forge that overlooks all of Birmingham. The sun was glinting off his big bare butt. Oh, yes. I was home.

I was waiting happily for Woofer to check out a telephone pole when a black Lincoln pulled up and stopped. I thought for a second that it was someone wanting directions, but when the window slid open, Pukey Lukey said, "Hey, Patricia Anne."

The sun was so bright, I couldn't see him well. I leaned through the window.

"Hey. What are you doing here? Debbie said you wanted to get in touch with us. I've been trying to call you."

Luke, I realized as my eyes adjusted, looked like he hadn't shaved in a couple of days. He was wearing dark glasses, but they weren't large enough to hide the puffiness beneath his eyes.

"What's wrong?" I was alarmed at his appearance. "Has something happened?"

"Oh, God, Patricia Anne. You wouldn't believe. Get in and let's go to your house. I was on the way there when I saw you."

This sounded bad, like something we would need time for. I looked down at Woofer who was now investigating the Lincoln's tires.

"You go on. I've got the dog. I'll be there in a minute."

"The dog's fine. You can put him in the backseat."

I looked at the maroon leather upholstery. Then I looked at Woofer.

"I think I'd better meet you there."

"All right. But hurry."

I straightened up, the window slid closed, and the black car pulled away from the curb right in front of a young man in a pickup who managed to slam on his brakes and shoot Luke a bird at the same time. Luke seemed unaware of the near collision and continued on down the street. The young man frowned at me.

"Sorry," I mouthed, as if I were to blame. I do this a lot, apologize for things that aren't my fault. I think it's because I've been Mary Alice's sister for sixty-one years.

We walked home faster than Woofer liked. He wanted to savor the trees and bushes more.

"We'll come back this afternoon," I assured him.

16

Luke's car was in our driveway and Luke was sitting on the back steps waiting. I took Woofer's leash off and he ambled over to investigate the strange man. Luke patted Woofer's head and began to cry. And for a second, I swear, this big man sitting on my back steps became the little boy crying because he had just thrown up all over everybody.

"Luke," I said, sitting down beside him and putting my arm around his shoulders. "What on earth's wrong?"

"Virginia." He reached in his pocket and pulled out a wad of wet tissue which he mopped his face with.

"What's wrong with her? Is she sick?"

He shook his head no. "She's left me."

"Virginia's left you?" I couldn't believe that was what he'd said.

"Gone. Skedaddled. Vamoosed." He tried to smile.

"But why? What's happened?" Virginia and Luke had been married for more than forty years. Fred and I had just started dating when I went to their wedding.

"Another man. She just up and ran off with another man, Patricia Anne." Luke buried his face in the wet tissue; his shoulders shook.

"Oh, surely not, Luke. Virginia wouldn't do that."

"Gone," he muttered into the tissue.

Woofer lay down across our feet. I pushed him off gently and took Luke's arm.

"Let's go in the house and get warm and get some coffee."

"I need to use the bathroom."

17

"Okay."

I was unlocking the door when Sister came through the gate.

"Hey, y'all," she said. "What's happening?"

I gave Luke a slight push as the door opened. "Go on to the bathroom." Then I waited for Sister.

"Was that Puke? Where did he go?"

"To the bathroom."

"To throw up?"

"I hope not. Come on in."

"Is something wrong?" She followed me into the kitchen.

"He says Virginia's left him."

"You're kidding. Why?"

"He says for another man. But I don't know any of the details. He just got here." I reached into the cabinet and got the coffee. "And he looks like hell, bless his heart."

"For another man? That's interesting." Sister sat down at the kitchen table.

"Interesting?" I measured the coffee into the Mr. Coffee.

"Sure. I wonder where she found him. Available men are as scarce as hen's teeth in Columbus."

I plugged in the coffeemaker and came to sit by her at the kitchen table. She was wearing a bright red sweatshirt printed with green frogs that leaped as she breathed. The effect was dizzying. Luke, I decided, given his predisposition to motion sickness, might be in trouble when confronted with this.

"Listen," I said. "He's very upset. And don't you dare call him Puke."

"You think I would be that rude?" The frogs jumped slightly.

"Just a reminder. You might forget."

"Well, I won't." She drummed red acrylic nails on my white table. "Reckon what he wants with us? I still bet it's politics and he wants money for Richard."

"I think he just wants somebody to talk to, and we're his only close relatives."

I was wrong, of course.

Luke looked slightly better when he came from the bathroom. He had combed his hair and probably splashed cold water on his face. It was less puffy. He still looked bad enough to shock Sister, though, who said, "Puke, you look like hell!"

He nodded sadly and sank down into the chair opposite me. "I know. I don't remember when I've slept." He took his first look at Sister and shut his eyes. "Mary Alice, are those frogs jumping?"

"I'll pull it off."

"Thank you."

She stood up, pulled the sweatshirt off, and folded it over the back of the chair.

"It's just a white shirt now."

"Thank you," Luke repeated and opened his eyes.

His appearance was startling. Even though he had several days' worth of beard, I could see his cheeks were sunken. Apparently he hadn't been eating either. I got up, turned on the oven, and got a package of Sister Schubert's orange rolls from the refrigerator.

"Patricia Anne says Virginia's run off with

19

another man," Sister said. No beating around the bush here.

Luke nodded. "She has. A man named Holden Crawford. A preacher who was painting our house."

"Holden Crawford? You're kidding. Sounds like *Catcher in the Rye*."

They both looked at me blankly. Neither of them would ever get on *Jeopardy!*

"Wait a minute," I said. "I want to hear this."

The coffee was made. I poured each of us a cup, put the rolls in the oven, and sat back down.

Luke put two teaspoons of sugar in his coffee and stirred it before he continued.

"It didn't take him but three days to paint the whole house, including the soffits. But when he left, Virginia went with him."

"What did he look like?" Sister wanted to know.

"I didn't pay much attention. Big. Dark hair." Luke sipped his coffee. "Every time I saw him, he was up on a ladder painting the soffits."

"And you're sure Virginia left with him?" I asked.

"She left me a note." Luke fished a piece of stationery from his shirt pocket and handed it to me. Across the top were flowers with babies peeking out of them. Written on it was: *Enough. I've gone with Holden.*

I handed the note to Sister.

"Cute stationery," she said.

Luke nodded. "I gave it to Virginia for her birthday. It looks like her. Beautiful and delicate."

I glanced at Luke's glasses. Nothing unusual about them. Not especially thick.

"She must have lost weight," Sister said. "Has she had cosmetic surgery recently?"

I aimed a kick at her ankles, but she had out-smarted me and was holding her legs up.

Luke was too upset to take offense. "She doesn't need it. When we went to the inaugural ball last year, nobody could believe she was Richard's mother." He sighed. "I just don't know what in the world got into her. Maybe religion. I know the man's a preacher."

I hopped up. "I'll get the sweet rolls."

"What kind of preacher is he?" Sister asked. "How come he's painting houses?"

"Doesn't make a living preaching, I guess. The man in Columbus who recommended him to do the painting says he's got a small church up near Gadsden. I can't even remember the name of it. Jesus Is Our Life and Heaven Hereafter or something like that. I'll bet it's a cult." Luke rubbed his hand across his eyes. "Oh, Lord. My sweet Virginia and poisoned Kool-Aid. And her a Lutheran." Luke sat up suddenly. "You don't suppose he kidnapped her, do you?"

Sister leaned forward. "How old is he?"

"Fiftyish."

"I doubt it seriously."

I was looking through the oven window, watching the icing melt on the sweet rolls. Poor Luke. I could understand his not wanting to admit that Virginia had just taken off with this Holden Crawford because she was smitten

21

with him. Holden Crawford. The English teacher inside me was smiling.

"Have you tried to get in touch with her?" I asked him.

"I went up to Gadsden. Nobody had heard of the church. There's no Holden Crawford listed in the phone book."

"There are a lot of Lutherans up there," Sister said. "Their families all came over from Germany. A lot of Catholics, too."

I tried to figure out if there was any point to this remark, decided there wasn't, and took the sweet rolls out of the oven.

"What I was hoping," Luke said as I handed each of them a plate and a napkin, "was if you two would help me."

"Help you how?" Sister reached for a sweet roll. "Ow. Hot." She stuck her finger in her mouth.

"Help me find Virginia."

"How could we do that?" I poured each of us more coffee.

"Well, we know the man's name and that he's a painter and a preacher. And we know his church is somewhere around Gadsden. Just because nobody that I asked in town knew him doesn't mean anything. We could check with the sheriff's office, branch out." He looked from me to Mary Alice who was already chewing orange roll and didn't look up.

I sat back down and reached for an orange roll. "Have you called Richard?"

Luke shook his head. "Didn't want to worry him."

"But look." Mary Alice held up her hand

for silence. We waited for her to swallow. "That's what children are for. I think, Luke, that you ought to call Richard and tell him that his mama's run off with a preacher who's a painter on the side and may have joined a cult. Tell him it's the Jesus' Open Hand church or whatever you said. Maybe the federal government has a file on them."

Luke blanched beneath the several days' growth of beard. "You think the federal government might have a file on this group?"

"Oh, sure. Every time you see one of those groups out waiting for the end of the world on a mountaintop, there's an FBI man right in the middle of them."

"Wait a minute," I said. This was fast getting out of control. "This Holden Crawford is a minister of a small church. Right?"

Luke and Sister agreed.

"The fact that it's a small church certainly doesn't mean it's a cult."

They nodded.

I continued. "He's attractive, in his fifties—"

"And he's up on a ladder painting the soffits," Sister interrupted. "What are soffits, anyway?"

"Those things under the eaves," Luke explained. He turned to me. "What are you getting at, Patricia Anne?"

"As I was saying—" I hesitated, expecting Sister to finish my sentence, but she didn't. "He's attractive, younger than Virginia. Maybe she was feeling a little lonesome."

"And there he was right outside her window reaching up to paint the soffits," Sister added.

Luke sighed. "I know, y'all. But she's my wife. I've got to know that she's all right."

"Well, eat an orange roll and let's think about this for a few minutes." I pushed the basket toward him.

Luke is a nice-looking man. The older he gets, the more I see a resemblance to my father, his uncle. Papa had a square jaw that neither Sister nor I inherited, but that Luke picked up from the Tate gene pool. Luke and Papa also had the same dark auburn hair, which had turned white by the time they were fifty. Luke's beard, I noticed as he leaned forward to take a roll, still had a lot of red in it. He had pulled off his jacket and was wearing a blue plaid flannel shirt that made his eyes, bloodshot as they were, look the same blue as Papa's. And the same blue as both of my boys. Damn.

Virginia has never been one of my favorite people. She's a "sizer-upper," one of those women who walks through your house and doesn't miss a thing. The kind who knows more about your medicine cabinet than you do.

But here was her husband, my papa's look-alike, sitting at my kitchen table asking me to help him. Saying he needed to know if she was all right.

Well, damn. What choice did I have?

"Tell us what we can do," I offered.

"Like I said, help me find her. She's been gone ten days."

"No problem," Sister said.

Chapter Three

Luke fell asleep on my guest room bed as soon as his head hit the pillow. He looked so sick, I wondered if we ought to take him to a doctor.

Sister said no. "He's just torn up about Virginia. Just goes to show."

She was still sitting at the kitchen table finishing up the last of the orange rolls.

"Show what?" I put Luke's coffee cup in the dishwasher and held up the coffee pot. She shook her head no, that she didn't want any more.

"That the man doesn't have biddy brains wanting that woman back. She puts on airs so, it's unbelievable."

I sat back down at the table.

"Virginia's not the most likable person in the world," I agreed. "But Luke loves her, and he's hurting."

Sister licked her finger and stuck it into the crumbs on the roll plate. Then she sucked the finger thoughtfully.

"I don't know what good finding her will do. She probably won't come back."

"Maybe not. But you told him we'd help, and he needs to know that she's all right."

"Sounds like she's better than all right."

I frowned at her and picked up the piece of paper on which I had written "Holden Crawford" and the name of his church, "Jesus Is Our Life and Heaven Hereafter." Beside the name of the church, I had put a question mark since Luke hadn't been sure that was right.

"You know," I said, "if the man lives near Gadsden, then we can look him up in that area. We can find him on the computer."

"And tell him to send Virginia home? Ha." Sister pushed her chair back. "I need to get the velvet bag you smuggled through customs."

"What?" The hair on my neck tingled. "I smuggled something through customs? You said it was your pearls and you forgot to put them with your jewelry."

"Well, it wasn't exactly my pearls. I don't guess it's smuggling, though, when it's right there and they don't pay any attention to it."

"You let me bring something in that could have gotten me in trouble? Arrested?"

"Oh, I knew you'd be all right. You look honest."

The only thing I had to throw at her was the piece of paper that I crumpled up.

"Well, don't get testy. Where's the bag? Still in your purse?"

"No. And whatever it is, I'm not going to give it to you, Miss Smarty."

"Why?" She looked genuinely puzzled at my reaction.

"Because it's mine since I'm the one smuggled it in. Whatever's in it is mine. What is it, anyway?"

"You don't want to know."

"Yes, I do."

"It's a testicle." Sister had put the sweat-shirt back on and the frogs were dancing again.

"What the hell do you mean, a testicle? You had me smuggle a body part into the country? My Lord, Mary Alice, where did you get a testicle?"

"From Philip. He sent it to Debbie." She motioned to a chair. "Sit down. It's not a real one. You probably didn't even break the law."

I sat and glared at her.

"You're pursing your lips," she said.

I didn't bother to answer.

"It's real simple," she continued. "They had some prosthetic testicles at the Warsaw medical school, but they were made out of silicone and they weren't using them any more. At least the surgeons weren't. But this obstetrician had a brainstorm. He'd give one to the women in labor to squeeze when they'd have a contraction. Philip said it worked wonders, cut the labor time in half."

"Are you serious? Philip sent Debbie a silicone testicle to squeeze when she's in labor?"

"He says it feels like the real thing. Has a marble or something in it." Sister looked at me. "Don't you wish you'd had one when you were in labor?"

"I wish they'd had epidurals when I was in labor."

"Well, I wish I'd had a testicle to squeeze, preferably Will Alec's, Roger's, or Philip's. There are times when a husband just isn't likable."

27

She pushed her chair back. "I'll just take it over to Debbie. She'll get a kick out of it. Philip says they call them Einstein's testicles."

"Why?" I couldn't believe I was actually interested in this.

"Proves the theory of relativity."

The woman had lost her mind. Our grandparents, Alice and John Tate, had three grandchildren, Luke, Mary Alice, and me. One out of three with good sense wasn't such a good average. And what made me think I had good sense? I'd spent the morning worrying with the other two.

Nevertheless, I went into my bedroom and got the little velvet bag from my nightstand. I squeezed it slightly and felt it give.

"Here," I said, handing it to Sister who was waiting by the back door. "Yuck."

"Thanks. And I really don't think you'd have been arrested."

I slammed the door behind her.

In November I had gotten an early Christmas present from Fred, an IBM Thinkpad. We had been gone for two weeks on our trip to Warsaw, so I had only had about a month to work with it. Just long enough to see the world that had been opened up for me.

Now, still fuming, I sat crosslegged on the bed and turned on the computer. Under WHITE PAGES, I typed Gadsden's regional area. Then I typed HOLDEN CRAWFORD. And there it was: HOLDEN R. CRAWFORD, R.R. 1, BOX 77, STEELE, AL. The phone number was also listed. Hot damn. So simple it was unbelievable.

I hadn't learned how to do the atlas on the Internet, so I went into the den and pulled down the Rand McNally. Steele. Near Gadsden. That town sounded familiar. I turned to the Alabama map, found Gadsden easily, and slightly southwest, Steele on Chandler Mountain. No wonder it had sounded familiar. The Steele exit was where we left I-59 when we went to arts-and-crafts festivals at Horse Pens 40, an unusual rock formation on the crest of the mountain. Every spring and fall they have three-day country-mountain celebrations there with blue grass music, clogging, and sorghum sopping with biscuits as large as plates. I'd never been into the town, but it couldn't be very large. Holden Crawford, I thought, should be easy to find.

"Good news," I told Luke when he shuffled into the den a couple of hours later. "I found Holden Crawford's address and phone number."

"How?" He sank into Fred's recliner. "You got any aspirin?"

"You wouldn't believe what you can find on a computer." I turned Oprah on mute, went into the kitchen, and came back with two aspirins and some water. "You need something to eat. These things will give you ulcers without food."

Luke gulped the aspirin down. "I've already got one. What's the phone number?"

I handed him the slip of paper I'd written the address and phone number on. "You going to call her now?"

29

"Might as well." He studied the address. "Where's Steele?"

"Not too far from Gadsden. Right off I-59. Why don't you go in the bedroom and call while I fix you a sandwich. Pimento cheese?"

"Okay." He got up, started toward the hall and paused. "What'll I say to her?"

"That you're worried about her and wanted to know she was all right."

"Oh. Okay."

I was pouring him a glass of milk when he came back.

"Nobody's at home." He sat down at the kitchen table and I put a sandwich and milk in front of him. "You sure that's Holden's number? The guy on the answering machine said, 'You've reached Monkey Man. Leave a message.' "

"Monkey Man? You're sure?"

"I swear that's what he said." Luke picked up his sandwich and looked at it as if he weren't sure what it was.

"It was the number listed in the computer white pages. Did you leave a message?"

"I said 'Virginia, if you're there, come home.' "

Not a message that would send Virginia galloping toward Columbus and Luke.

"You didn't say you were missing her and worried about her?"

"Patricia Anne, I was talking to a someone named Monkey Man." Luke sighed and bit into his sandwich. The afternoon sun glinted off of his reddish beard as he chewed. I thought that maybe I should offer him one of the razors that I shave my legs with. I buy them ten to a package since Fred acts like such a fool if I use his razor. There were some new toothbrushes in the medicine cabinet, too. Luke would feel better with a shower and some grooming.

He looked up and saw me watching him.

"What?" he asked.

"I was just thinking how much you look like Papa."

He smiled, making the resemblance even more pronounced.

"Luke," I said. "You really might ought to call Richard." Really might ought? Lord, we Southerners do have a way with words.

He shook his head. "Don't want to worry him unless I have to."

"Well, I can appreciate that. But it's been how long since Virginia left? Ten days?"

He nodded and stuck the last bite of sandwich in his mouth.

"Richard would want to know, I'm sure."

"No. That boy's got enough on his shoulders. He's got the government to run."

Hey. I watch C-SPAN. I know how many of those representatives are there on any given day. But Luke, bless his heart, was serious.

"I'm going to find out exactly where she is and what's going on before I bother him." He reached in his pocket and pulled out the piece of paper that I had written Holden Crawford's address and phone number on. "How far is it to Steele?"

"I can show you." I opened the atlas and

pointed to Steele. "It's on Chandler Mountain."

"That's not that close to Gadsden," he said. "Maybe it's not the right Holden Crawford."

"The computer lists it in the Gadsden area, Luke. And Holden Crawford isn't a common name. I'll bet it's him."

He pushed his chair back. "Well, it's not but about an hour's drive. I guess I'd better go check it out."

Not but about. Two weeks of communicating with gestures and simple words in Warsaw and I'm drowning in extra words.

"Wait, Luke," I said. "You don't know where you're going and you don't want to be wandering around up there on those dark mountainous roads. Besides, you're tired. Keep calling, and if you still don't get an answer, I'll ride up there with you in the morning."

He looked at me doubtfully.

"A good supper and a good night's sleep, and you'll feel a lot better."

And so would I. My body was still halfway across the Atlantic.

"Okay. I'll try to call again in a few minutes."

What had I let myself in for?

The back door opened and Mary Alice stuck her head in.

"I forgot my gloves."

"Did you take Debbie her testicle?"

"She wasn't at home."

"It's a miracle I didn't get arrested."

"Oh, don't be silly. The customs folks gave

32

you one look and said, 'Welcome home, Miss Honest Citizen.' " She stepped into the kitchen and closed the door.

"Testicle?" Luke asked.

"It's a long story. Get Mary Alice to explain it to you." I got up, put on my coat, and went to take Woofer for a walk. The cold air felt wonderful.

Fred, Luke, and I had waffles and turkey bacon for supper. We ate in the den in front of the fire while Fred listened carefully to the story of the missing Virginia. Too carefully, I realized, when I heard a slight snore from his corner of the sofa. Luke, however, didn't seem to notice that he had lost half his audience. He kept talking while I collected the plates and put a pillow under Fred's head. He was still talking nonstop an hour and a half later, God knows about what, when I got Fred up and took him off to bed. I was beginning to understand why Virginia had skedaddled off with the soffit painter.

"I'm going up to Steele in the morning with Luke," I told Fred as I crawled in beside him. It was very late. At least 8:30.

"Fine," he said. "Have a good time."

The last thing I remembered that night was Muffin jumping up on the bed between us.

ChapterFour

E-MAIL
FROM: **HALEY**
TO: **MAMA**
SUBJECT: ANGELS

Of course I believe in angels, Mama.
  I love you,
   Haley

E-MAIL
FROM: **MAMA**
TO: **HALEY**
SUBJECT: BALLS

Honey, is your Aunt Sister lying to me or did Philip give her a silicone testicle for Debbie to squeeze when she's in labor? She said it was her pearls and put it in my purse which, fortunately, the customs people didn't search. I could wring her neck. Pukey Lukey is here, Virginia has run off with a house painter who lives up at Steele. That's the little town where you exit to go to Horse Pens 40. Remember? Where we bought your Log Cabin quilt. Anyway, we're going up there today. He says he just wants to know that she's okay. He showed up yesterday looking like the wrath of God. She's been gone ten days. We told him to call Richard, but he says Richard is too busy running the government, a scary thought. I'll keep you posted.

How was the party?

I miss you.

Love,

Mama

As I turned off the computer, I heard the toilet in the hall bathroom flush. It was 8:30, Fred had gone to work and I had been up an hour, but we had been quiet so Luke could sleep. There was no hurry about going to Steele.

I knocked on the guest room door and handed Luke a toothbrush and a razor. He was buttoning the blue plaid shirt he had worn the day before and I considered offering him one of Fred's, but decided it would be too small for him. A week of worrying hadn't lessened Luke's belly.

"There's coffee when you're ready," I said.

"Thanks."

"An egg?"

"Just some cereal."

I went into the kitchen and picked Muffin up from the table. Out of the bay window, I could see the bare limbs of the trees bending in the wind. Dark gray clouds were layered across the sky. If this weren't Birmingham, Alabama, and if I hadn't just heard the weatherman say it was going to be partly cloudy, I would have sworn it was going to snow. I checked the thermometer on the deck. Thirty-eight degrees. No sign of Woofer. He was taking full advantage of his igloo doghouse, one of the best buys I ever made.

"Looks like a raw day," Luke said when he came in.

"Looks like snow," I agreed. "But the weatherman says it's not going to. He says it's going to be partly cloudy."

Luke looked better, probably because he had shaved.

I held up Cheerios and corn flakes. He pointed to the Cheerios. I poured some in two bowls and cut up half a banana in each.

"Thanks." Luke picked up a spoon and began to eat silently, glancing occasionally out of the bay window. Somehow this worried me more than the nonstop talk of the day before.

"I could fix us some sandwiches to take," I offered, finishing my cereal. "Turkey? Ham?"

He nodded, though I was sure my words hadn't scored a hit. Wherever Luke's thoughts were, they weren't in my kitchen.

I got the sandwich makings out of the refrigerator and was spreading mayonnaise on a slice of bread when Luke said, "I think Virginia's dead, Patricia Anne."

"Oh, Luke, of course she's not. Don't even think like that. We're going to find her today."

"No, we're not."

There was a finality in his voice that made me look up. He was staring out of the window, both hands clasped around a coffee mug.

Did he know more than he had told us? Had sixty-three-year old Virginia run off with a house painter or had something else happened? How well did we really know Luke? We saw him at family weddings and funerals, exchanged Christmas and birthday cards.

I slapped a slice of turkey on the bread and told myself I was crazy, still jet-lagged. This was Pukey Lukey, our cousin, for heaven's sake. Nevertheless, I jumped when Luke pushed his chair back. He came over, put his mug in the dishwasher, and gave me a hug.

"Thanks."

"You're welcome." The hug was sweet, appreciative. What on God's earth had I been thinking?

"I'm going to call that phone number one more time," he said. "What kind of a person would call himself Monkey Man?"

I shrugged. I had just seen Sister coming up the back steps. "Is she going with us?"

"I asked her yesterday. That's okay, isn't it?"

"Fine." Given the thoughts that were zipping through my brain all morning, it was more than fine. "I'll fix some more sandwiches."

"Lord, it's cold. Y'all ready? I swear I think it's going to snow." Sister swept in dressed in a dark purple cape which looked like a purple blanket with slits for the arms. Add to that purple boots. The Fruit of the Loom people would have hired her in a minute for a commercial.

"That's some outfit," Luke said.

Sister twirled. "Warsaw. I haven't seen anything like it here."

I hadn't seen anything like it in Warsaw.

"Pour yourself a cup of coffee," I said. "We'll be ready in a minute."

"I've got us a whole thermos of coffee in the car."

The first look of pleasure that I'd seen since Luke had gotten here lit up his face. "You're going to let me ride in your Jaguar?"

The woman didn't miss a beat. "I think your car would be more comfortable."

An hour and a half later we pulled into a parking place at the Steele post office. We had decided on the way up the interstate that this was the only way to find Holden Crawford since all we had was a rural route address.

Urban sprawl from Birmingham has not reached Steele. With the exception of the modern post office and a cutesy tearoom painted blue, the one downtown street was lined with buildings that had been there for a century. Unlike many small Alabama towns, though, Steele seemed to be holding its own. Most of the buildings were well maintained and, most important, occupied by businesses. The sidewalks weren't crowded, but neither were they empty. There was even a grocery store that was not part of a large chain. Several cars were parked in front of it.

"I'll go ask," Luke said.

We watched him go up the steps; the wind whipped against him and he covered his ears with his hands.

"Nice town," I said. "Did you see the public library in that elegant old house?"

"The tearoom looked good." Sister turned

and pointed toward the basket on the seat beside me. "Hand me a sandwich. I'm hungry."

"What kind?"

"Doesn't matter. I hope Puke's not in there long. It's already getting cold in here." She had draped the purple cape over the back of the seat. Now she pulled it around her shoulders and looked at the Ziploc bag I had given her. "There's nothing runny in these sandwiches, is there? I don't want to mess up this outfit."

"Just turkey or ham."

She unwrapped it and took a bite. "Turkey."

I leaned forward and propped my arms on the back of the front seat.

"Did Luke tell you that Holden Crawford's answering machine says you've reached Monkey Man? This whole thing is weird. You know? Can you imagine Virginia running off with a man called Monkey Man?"

Sister chewed thoughtfully and swallowed. "I can't imagine a man called Monkey Man running off with Virginia. In fact, I can't imagine any man running off with Virginia."

"I can't either," I said truthfully. "That's one thing that's worrying me about this whole affair."

"On the other hand, she's just in her sixties. I guess it could have been eyes across a crowded room. Or through the window, in this case. Who knows?" Sister took another bite of sandwich. "Maybe she's been doubling up on her estrogen." She chewed. "I wonder if that works?"

"Maybe something's happened to her and Luke knows it and isn't telling us."

"You're crazy."

Jet-lagged to hell and back, anyway.

Luke came out of the post office, plowing through the wind and the debris that was skittering along the steps.

"Lord!" he said, slamming the door. "It's going to snow sure as anything."

"What did you find out?" Sister asked.

"You follow the signs up to Horse Pens 40. It's about a half a mile past the Horse Pens's entrance. A white house on the left, right by a church. Probably the church where he preaches."

Luke started the car and cold air blasted us.

"It'll be warm in a minute," he apologized. "Which way is Horse Pens 40?"

"Go back to where we came into town. You'll see the signs." Back to where?

"The man in the post office laughed when I asked for Holden Crawford. He said, 'You talking about Monk?' I said I guessed so."

"Well, Monk doesn't sound so bad," Sister said. She pointed toward the tearoom. "Why don't we stop for lunch?"

"I've got to find Virginia first."

I handed Sister another sandwich.

As she was unwrapping it, she asked, "Luke, do you know how much estrogen Virginia takes?"

"She doesn't need it."

Sister and I looked at each other. Silence does have a sound.

We stopped at a four-way stop. A pickup with

40

two bird dogs in the back turned left and headed up Chandler Mountain ahead of us. The dogs didn't seem to be uncomfortable. They were sitting against the cab, leaning into the curves as the truck climbed the mountain. I knew they were cold, though, and I knew the open bed of a pickup was no place for an animal. I was relieved when the driver put on his turn signal and turned into the driveway of a farmhouse.

Chandler Mountain is a series of plateaus, some so wide you can't tell you're up high. The land is rich and well farmed. The area is known for its pimentos and tomatoes, which ripen well into November. Something about the thermals delays frost there for several weeks.

Winter had come with a vengeance that day in January, though. We passed a huge tomato-packing shed. A sign that proclaimed this was a farmer's co-op had come loose on one side and twisted in the wind. There was nothing that hinted that this had been a busy place just two months earlier.

The plateau ended, and the road became a series of sharp curves. There was little traffic. The only car we met was going slowly and was barely on its side of the road, the bluff side with no guardrails. The driver, an old bearded man, waved at us.

"Who the hell would want to live up here?" Luke grumbled.

"It's beautiful when you get to the top," I said. "You can stand on the rocks at Horse Pens and see forever. The most beautiful sunsets you ever saw."

"How come they call it Horse Pens 40?"

"The rocks form a natural corral. The Indians used to herd their horses in there, so they say. The 40 is because it's the forty-acre parcel that Horse Pens is on."

We had reached another plateau and passed by the entrance to Horse Pens where a sign attached to a barbwire fence announced that the spring festival would be April 22, 23, 24.

"Start looking for the house," Luke said. "The mailbox, anyway."

There were several small houses, all close to the road. Except for the smoke coming from chimneys, there were no signs of people. Occasionally in frostbitten gardens, a few turnip greens still showed color.

Sister pointed. "There. There's a church."

Luke slowed down.

The house next to the church sat farther back from the road than most of its neighbors, but like the others, it was small, two rooms wide with a narrow porch. Its only distinguishing feature was that in the front yard was a large satellite dish. On the mailbox was the name CRAWFORD.

Luke turned left into the gravel driveway between the church and house and stopped.

"What's the matter?" Sister asked. "This has got to be the right place. Look. There's a van with ladders and stuff on it."

"I don't know. I don't feel so good." Luke leaned his head against the steering wheel.

"He's just nervous," I said to Sister. And then to Luke, "Aren't you?"

"What if she doesn't want to see me?" he said, his head still down.

"Then she's crazy. There's everything in Columbus. Malls, department stores. Up here," Sister pointed to the satellite dish, "they don't even have cable TV."

"But she left me, Mary Alice."

"And you have come to her rescue." Sister turned and looked at me. "Isn't that right, Mouse?"

"I guess so. You need to talk to her, anyway, Luke."

What looked suspiciously like a tear dripped down the steering wheel.

"I tell you what," I offered. "I'll go see if she's here. How about that?"

"Would you? I don't want to see that Crawford guy."

"Sure."

I opened the car door and looked across the yard carefully. In spite of the church next door, this looked like pit bull territory. Nothing moved on the porch or darted from under the house. Nevertheless, I armed myself with an umbrella I had found on the backseat before I marched across the yard to knock on the door.

No one answered.

I knocked again, even calling, "Virginia?"

Still no answer. I looked in the window of what was the living room. It was furnished with a sofa and a giant TV, one of those that's so big the picture is blurry.

I looked back at the car and shrugged at Luke and Mary Alice. Then I moved over and looked into the bedroom. It was neat, the bed made up with a pink chenille bedspread.

I tapped on the window. Nothing.

"They're not here," I said to Luke and Mary Alice as I got back in the car. "I swear I think I saw a snowflake, though."

"But his truck's here. Maybe they're over there." Luke pointed toward the church.

"Well, you go look." I pulled my coat collar up. If that really had been a snowflake, we wouldn't be able to stay up on Chandler Mountain long. In Warsaw it had been business as usual over Christmas despite a foot of snow on the ground and more falling all the time. In Alabama, a dusting of snow totally incapacitates us. And that's on the flat areas.

"He could have an office over there," Sister said.

I looked at the church. Small, white paint peeling, it was probably one large room. This was a country church, built like the houses around it. There wouldn't be room for ministers' offices or choir lofts, just a row of wooden benches and perhaps a raised platform for the preacher.

"Okay, I'll go see." Luke got out of the car and marched toward the church.

"There's nothing over there," I said to Sister.

"Probably not. Here." She handed me a Styrofoam cup of coffee. "This'll warm you up."

I took the coffee gratefully and felt the steam rise against my cold face.

"He's going in," Sister said. "The door was unlocked."

There were double doors at the front of the church. As I looked up, Luke disappeared through the one on the right.

"I hope he hurries," I said. "We need to get off this mountain."

"We sure do. I've got a museum board meeting tonight." She took her cell phone from her purse. "I'm going to check on Debbie."

"Did you give her her present?"

"I thought I'd take it over this afternoon."

I sipped my coffee and looked out at the gray day. A couple more snowflakes drifted by. I closed my jet-lagged eyes. Sister's conversation with Debbie seemed far away.

"Debbie says they're predicting snow showers," Sister said.

I jumped. A little coffee sloshed on my corduroy pants. Damn. Not a good idea going to sleep holding hot coffee.

"We need to go. Reckon what Puke's doing in there anyway?"

"Praying?" I was still half asleep.

"Don't be ridiculous, Mouse. It's too cold. Come on. Let's go get him."

To this day I don't know why I got out of the car and followed her across the church-yard, still clutching my coffee. The habit of sixty years, I suppose.

Sister opened the church door and called, "Luke?"

There was no answer, and she walked in. I was right behind her.

45

There were windows down both sides of the church, which, as I had surmised, was one large room. So we could see, and what we could see was that there was no Luke in the place.

"Luke?" Sister called again, walking up the aisle.

A strange sound, a moan, made us both stop.

"What the hell was that?" Sister whispered.

"How the hell do I know?" I whispered back. "And don't talk like that in church."

"Luke?" Sister's voice was hesitant.

Again the moan.

"He's sick," I said. I brushed past Sister to the front pew.

An unconscious Luke lay there on the floor, blood pouring from a deep cut on his forehead.

I was cool. I had taught school for thirty years. I carefully placed my coffee on the bench, knelt beside Luke, and felt the pulse in his neck. I knew from my in-service training that this was what I was supposed to do. I don't know why. He was obviously alive.

"Get me something like a towel," I told Sister. "And some water."

"Oh, my God, Mouse. Look behind you."

I turned. Lying on the front pew across the aisle was a woman. Though she was on her stomach, her neck was twisted so far around that bright red hair fell across her face and brushed the floor.

"Is she dead?" Sister whispered.

Of course she was. Nobody's head fit their neck that way.

"Of course she is."

"Oh, God. I'm going to be sick." Sister ran down the aisle and threw the door open.

As I said, I was cool. I don't fall apart during emergencies. I pulled off my coat and my sweatshirt, put my coat back on, and pressed the sweatshirt against Luke's forehead. Behind me, the dead girl's eyes stared at the ceiling.

It was January, I thought. Bed Bath & Beyond were having a wonderful sale. Those big towels that were like sheets. Fred would like that. And one of those George Foreman grills. Maybe they were on sale, too. This afternoon when we got home, I'd go right over to the Summit and see. No problem.

Chapter Five

I'm not sure how long I wandered the aisles of Bed Bath & Beyond before I heard the church door creak open. Probably only a few minutes.

Mary Alice came in and sat on the back bench.

"I called 911," she said.

"Okay."

"You doing your Martha Stewart bit?"

She knows me too well.

"Beats throwing up." I lifted the sweatshirt and looked at Luke's forehead. The bleeding had almost stopped, but my sweat-shirt had soaked up a lot of blood.

"Luke?" I said. "Luke, answer me."

His eyes fluttered, and he moaned. I sat back on my heels and looked at the way he was lying, crumpled on his side. I'd had to turn his head to staunch the bleeding. Had he fallen and hit his head on the bench or had he been attacked? Maybe he had seen the woman's body and fainted. He'd said he wasn't feeling well.

I glanced over at the dead woman. Whoever had broken her neck had laid her out on the bench as if she were sleeping. She was wearing a long, blue-flowered challis skirt and a white blouse. Her skirt had been neatly tucked around black boots whose soles were encrusted with red clay. And she had to be young from the appearance of the coppery mass of hair cascading to the floor.

Damn. I shivered.

I was about to return to the white sales at Bed Bath & Beyond when Mary Alice announced that the 911 people would be there in a few minutes. And did I know where the nearest hospital was?

"Oneonta?" I guessed. "Gadsden?" I pressed my fingers against Luke's pulse again. Was it my imagination or was it thready? "I hope not far. I think Luke's going into shock. Bring me your cape. We've got to get him warm."

"It'll get blood on it."

"Damn it, Sister!"

She came down the aisle slowly and side-ways so she wouldn't see the woman's body.

48

"He doesn't look good, does he?" she said, handing me the cape. "Luke? You okay?" She yelled the latter as if deafness were Luke's problem.

I took the cape, spread it over Luke, and added my coat.

"He came in while the murderer was still here, didn't he? And the murderer tried to kill him."

"I doubt it." I pointed toward the woman. "I think she's been dead awhile. Look at her hand hanging over the bench. It's almost black. I don't know what you call that, but it's got a name, where the blood seeps down to the lowest part."

Sister turned green and dashed from the church again. Served her right.

Luke opened his eyes and then closed them again. I rubbed his arms and hands. I needed something to elevate his legs. Hymnals, I thought. But there weren't any in the church.

From a distance there was the welcome sound of a siren. Then it died out. And then I heard it again. Coming up the mountain, I realized, the hairpin curves breaking the sound.

The door opened.

"They're coming," Sister announced. "I'll flag them down."

The sound was steady now. They were crossing the Horse Pens plateau, beginning their descent toward the church. And then they were pulling into the driveway where I could hear Sister yelling, "This way!"

I held Luke's hand and waited.

Three large men dressed in uniforms rushed

through the door and then stopped so suddenly they almost fell over each other.

"Lady, you by yourself?" one of them asked.

"What?"

"The snakes up?"

"We're not coming no farther less they are," a second one said.

"What are you talking about? There's a hurt man here and a dead woman."

"No snakes?"

"Of course not. What's the matter with you?"

"Just making sure," the first man said. "Come on, y'all."

I moved aside. They glanced at the dead woman and then concentrated on Luke. Blood pressure cuffs came out. Heart monitors. One of the men was talking on a cell phone, nodding, receiving information from a trauma center, I realized, where this information was being transmitted. I was impressed.

"Here." One of the paramedics handed me my coat and Sister's cloak. She had followed the men into the church and was sitting on a back bench. I took the cloak back to her and put my own coat on.

"Did you hear them asking about snakes?"

"No." She shivered. "It's snowing. I swear, Patricia Anne. I can't figure out for the life of me how you keep getting us into these predicaments."

"Me? Ha!" A real smart answer and the end of that conversation. We huddled on the bench in silence.

In a few minutes we heard another siren. Two deputy sheriffs came in, spoke to the paramedics, and started working the other side of the aisle where the woman's body was.

"What a mess," Sister grumbled.

I got up and walked outside. It was, indeed, snowing. Tiny, dry flakes were being blown by the wind. Lord, we needed to get off this mountain.

An ambulance pulled up. Two young women hopped out, nodded to me, and rushed into the church.

"Mouse?"

Sister was standing in the doorway.

"The policemen want to talk to you."

"Why? All we did was ride up here with Luke to look for Virginia."

"That's what I told them."

"Lady?" One of the paramedics leaned around Sister. "We're taking your husband to the hospital in Oneonta. You want to ride in the ambulance?"

I didn't bother to explain that Luke wasn't my husband.

"Of course. How is he?"

"We've got him pretty stable."

The two young women came out lifting Luke down the steps as if he weighed nothing. He had regained consciousness, but looked puzzled.

"Patricia Anne?" he said when he saw me.

"I'm going to ride in the ambulance with you, Luke."

"Where's Virginia?"

"She'll be along later," I lied.

"What about the policemen?" Sister called as I followed the gurney.

"I don't have anything to tell them."

The ambulance doors closed, and I got the hell off of Chandler Mountain.

All ambulance drivers should be women. The one who was actually doing the driving took the hairpin curves gently. The other woman sitting in the back with Luke and me introduced herself as Tammy Parsons. Around thirty and pretty with dark curly hair, she held Luke's hand and told us about the new house she and her husband were building up near Gadsden on the river. A real log cabin from a kit.

"Must be a big kit," Luke said.

Tammy smiled. "Now, aren't you doing fine."

"Luke? You awake enough to tell me what happened?" I asked.

"I saw Virginia."

"In the church?"

"Yes. In the church."

I leaned closer because his voice was getting fainter.

"Are you sure it was Virginia? What happened? Did you fall and hit your head?"

There was no answer.

"He's gone again," Tammy said, checking gauges. "He's okay, though. If he's got a fractured skull, it'll be tomorrow that we have to worry about. The swelling."

I could have done without that news.

"How long have y'all been married?" Tammy asked.

"We're not. He's my cousin."

"He one of the snake handlers?"

"What?"

"At the church. Is he one of the snake handlers? We get called up there every now and then. Last time the fellow's arm was the size of an elephant's leg, I swear, before they called. Wasn't much we could do for him. Course he'd been drinking strychnine, too."

Tammy looked up and saw the expression on my face. I'm sure my mouth was open.

"What?" she asked. "Y'all aren't handlers?"

I found my voice. "Of snakes? Good God, no."

"Well, I just figured maybe you were since you were at the Jesus Is Our Life and Heaven Hereafter church."

I was having trouble breathing. "People handle snakes there?"

"Oh, sure." She studied me. "You really didn't know?"

I shook my head no.

"Didn't you see that box at the front? That's where they keep the snakes."

And the paramedics had seen that box and that was why they were falling over each other wanting to know if the snakes were up. And I hadn't put two and two together.

My Lord. I put my head down on the gurney. It was too surreal. Four days ago, I had been on the Concorde zipping back from

Europe. Today I was riding in an ambulance down Chandler Mountain from a snake-handling church.

"You okay, ma'am?" Tammy asked.

"I think so." I just hoped the ambulance didn't have too many more curves to swing around.

"They say that Chandler Mountain has the most and the biggest rattlesnakes in the world," Tammy said proudly. "I wonder if that woman in the church was bit."

Not even thoughts of a sale at Bed Bath & Beyond could rescue me, especially when Tammy said, "Your cousin here looks like the Chandler Mountain booger got a hold of him."

"The Chandler Mountain booger?"

"Yes, ma'am. You never heard of it?"

I shook my head no; Tammy seemed surprised.

"Sort of a cross between a bear and a wildcat. I've never seen it, but lots of folks up here have. It makes an ungodly noise. Kind of a whine and a screech and a moan all at one time." Tammy shook her head. "You don't want to get in the way of the booger. No, ma'am."

For a moment I thought she was teasing, trying to see how much a naive flatland foreigner would believe.

"A cross between a bear and a wildcat?"

"Oh, yes, ma'am. You hear that noise, you want to get away quick."

She was serious.

The staff of the Blount County Medical Center emergency room was expecting us. Luke was whisked off and I was ushered into a small glass cubicle to answer all of the questions that I could.

"Bye." Tammy stuck her head in the doorway. "She don't know about the snakes, Irene. The booger, neither."

Irene waved. "Just as well, Tammy. Bye."

Irene was a middle-aged woman whose head fit right on her shoulders. Whoever had broken the girl's neck at the church would have had trouble with Irene. I shivered, pushing the thought aside.

"You want some coffee, Mrs. Nelson?"

I nodded. We'd get the name straightened out soon enough. When Irene got up, I saw that she was built like a box. Not only was there no neck, there was no discernible waist. She was back in a moment with a Styrofoam cup of coffee, though, and the nicest smile. Irene, I decided gratefully, was the perfect person for this job, sturdy and comforting.

It took several minutes after I explained to her that I was Luke's cousin, not his wife, for her to locate his insurance cards. She called the treatment room where they had taken him, and a nurse brought Luke's wallet out. Irene had me go through it to find his cards. The first card I pulled out was his driver's license. Luke looked startled in the picture. Vulnerable. I suddenly felt like crying.

"Here." I handed Irene the insurance card.

"Trash!" she said.

"Blue Cross?"

"Of course not. Look what just walked in. Don't turn around. Just look."

Between jet lag and everything that had already happened that day, I was totally confused.

"What?"

"Well, just turn around a little bit and look. You won't believe this."

A tall bearded man had walked into the emergency room. He was wearing a black short-sleeved T-shirt that had KILL THEM ALL. LET GOD SORT THEM OUT emblazoned in large white letters below a death's head that was wearing a pirate's hat.

"My God!"

He was here to rob the emergency room of its drugs. And there was nothing between us and his semiautomatic but glass. This was it. This was Death. I waited.

Death sat down and glanced through a *Southern Living* magazine.

"Comes in here every afternoon to pick up his wife," Irene sniffed. "She's nice as she can be. One of our best nurses. Just no sense."

My heart began to beat again. I could feel it drumming against my ribs.

"Well, it's none of my business she wants to be a fool," Irene said. She picked up the card. "Okay, let's see what we've got here."

The outside door opened again and two young women came in brushing off their coats.

"It's snowing, Irene," one of them called as they headed down the hall.

Irene waved in their direction. "Snow. Just what we need."

I thought of the hairpin curves on Chandler Mountain. Surely the policemen would let Sister leave before the roads got too icy.

"Things ice up around here in a second," Irene said as if she were reading my mind. "Causes all kinds of problems."

Guilt. I had left my sister on top of a booger-occupied mountain in a snowstorm in a snake-handling church with a dead body.

"What happened to your cousin?" Irene asked.

"I'm not sure. We were at this church up on Chandler Mountain, and he went in to look for his wife, and when he didn't come back we went in to look for him and he was unconscious and bleeding and there was a dead woman on the bench across from him. A dead woman with a lot of red hair and a broken neck." I paused for breath.

"Is that right?" Irene pushed some papers toward me. "Here, sign these."

"Her head was on backward."

"Have mercy." Irene handed me a ballpoint pen. "Sign right here and," she lifted the top sheet of paper, "here."

I signed.

"Okay," she glanced at my signature, "Mrs. Hollowell. Somebody will be out in a little while when they find out what's what with your cousin."

Backward heads didn't seem to make much

of an impression on Irene. They sure as hell did on me, though. I sat in the waiting room with my teeth chattering. Fortunately Death had left with his pretty young wife, who had fussed at him for not wearing a jacket.

I wondered how Luke was doing. I wondered what had happened to him. The most reasonable scenario I could come up with was that he had seen the dead girl, fainted, and hit his head on the corner of the bench. That made sense. And he had been talking out of his head when he said he had seen Virginia. We had been sitting in front in the car and hadn't seen anyone come out of the church.

But there was a back door. I closed my eyes and tried to remember the details. On the right-hand side was a door and if anyone had left that way, we wouldn't have been able to see them. I remembered thinking that the door should have been on the other side, the side that the house was on so the preacher wouldn't have to walk around the back.

Holden Crawford. Monk Crawford. Lord, how had Virginia Nelson who played golf at the country club in Columbus and who had a son in the House of Representatives gotten mixed up with a snake-handling preacher?

I thought of the box at the front. Surely there weren't any snakes in there now. It was cold in the church. Snakes hibernate. But would that matter? Drowsy snakes might be better to deal with. Unless, of course, they hated to be awakened. A riled rattlesnake would be a challenge.

And it didn't make sense that someone had killed the girl so violently and then laid her out neatly on a church bench. They could have dumped her almost anywhere on Chandler Mountain and she would never have been found. They could have walked out on one of numerous rocky precipices and thrown the body into a sea of kudzu that would have covered her forever. Instead, there she was on a pew at the Jesus Is Our Life and Heaven Hereafter church, her long skirt tucked neatly around her boots.

I glanced at my watch. I was going to have to call Fred in a little while. There was no way I was going to make it home before he did and he would be worried. I got up and looked outside. The snow was coming down steadily. Fine, dry flakes that looked like rain. The streets were still clear, but the grass beside the emergency room parking lot was beginning to turn white.

Lord, I was tired. I stretched but snapped to attention when Luke's Lincoln pulled into the parking lot. Mary Alice stepped out, purple hood over her head (I hadn't realized the cape had a hood) and hurried toward the emergency room. I opened the door for her. Might as well get the fussing over with. After all, I had left her up on the mountain to deal with the police and a dead body.

"Hello, sweetie," she said, hugging me. "How's Luke?"

Let the record be clear here. In sixty-one years I never remember my sister calling me sweetie. And the hug was so unexpected, that I breathed and was nearly overcome by White Diamonds perfume.

"I haven't heard," I said when I could breathe. "He's in the back."

"Well, is there a cafeteria or something around here? I'm starving." She looked around at the waiting room and the glass cubicle where Irene was still on duty. "This isn't a very busy emergency room, is it?"

"Maybe it will pick up after a while if the roads get slick."

"Maybe," she agreed. Sarcasm is lost on Sister.

"Excuse me." She stuck her head around the door of the glass cubicle. "Could you tell us where to get something to eat?"

"Joe's," Irene answered.

"And here in the hospital?"

"Some vending machines down the hall."

"Thanks. We'd better stay here. We're waiting for the sheriff."

"Why are you in such a good humor?" I ventured.

"I'm not." Sister sat down and started rummaging through her purse. "You got any change?"

"The vending machines will make change."

"Of course they will. What am I thinking of?"

I was damned if I knew. She was acting weird.

She handed me several one-dollar bills. "Get me some kind of sandwich and potato chips and a Coke."

"Okay." I wasn't about to push my luck and tell her to get it herself.

I found the vending machines and got back with the food just in time to see the reason for Sister's good mood. The emergency room door opened and a man in uniform swept in. He looked a lot like Gen. Norman Schwarzkopf with a little Willard Scott thrown in. He paused, Sister got up, and then they walked toward each other. I swear if this had been a movie they would have been playing something like "Unchained Melody" in the background.

They stopped about a foot apart and smiled.

"I got pimento cheese," I said. "Is that all right?"

"Mouse," Sister said. "This is Virgil Stuckey, the sheriff of St. Clair County. Sheriff, this is my sister, Patricia Anne Hollowell."

He turned to shake my hand, realized I was balancing Cokes and sandwiches, and said, "Here, let me help you."

Sister pushed magazines to one end of a coffee table and we put the food down. She and I sat on the sofa and Virgil Stuckey pulled up a chair.

"Do you know, Mary Alice," he said admiringly. "I don't think I've ever seen purple boots before."

The man was hooked.

Chapter Six

E-MAIL
FROM: HALEY
TO: MAMA

Philip says the testicle is called a neutercal, which sounds nutritious, like some kind of a drink with vitamins. He says obstetricians swear by them here. Debbie says she will send me a picture of David Anthony on the Internet right after he's born. The hospital does it somehow. I can't wait to see him.

I hope your jet lag is fine by now. I finally got an E-mail from Alan. He says they're fine and had a good Christmas. Thank the Lord he came to his senses and he and Lisa are doing okay. They are, aren't they?

We are. Last night we rented *Fargo* and had popcorn and hot chocolate.

Any news?

Give Papa a kiss for me. Aunt Sister, too.

I love you all.

Haley

Any news? I turned off the computer. Maybe later in the day I would have time to tell Haley all that had happened. In the meantime, I had to get dressed and go back up to Oneonta. I had checked with the hospital, and they were releasing Luke in the afternoon.

It had been almost ten o'clock the night before when we got home. We wanted to talk to the doctors and be sure Luke was all right. No fracture, they assured us, but a bad concussion. They wanted to keep him twenty-four hours for observation.

Virgil Stuckey had torn himself away from admiring Sister's purple boots long enough to ask Luke some questions. Yes, Luke had seen Virginia in the church. That was all he remembered. His head hurt and how come he couldn't open his eyes good?

"You hit your head," the sheriff told him. "There's a bandage on your forehead and your eyes are swollen."

"Why would I hit myself on the head?"

"We think you fell."

"Oh. Okay." Luke closed his eyes and went back to sleep.

"I'll need statements from both of you," Sheriff Stuckey informed Mary Alice and me. "We can do it over dinner at Joe's."

We walked about a block through fine, powdery snow to Joe's Family Restaurant. My statement, told while we were waiting for our dinner (fried chicken, mashed potatoes, and green beans), was that I had gone into the church, found Luke unconscious and bleeding, and tried to stem the bleeding. And yes, I had seen the dead woman lying on the bench.

Sister's statement over pieces of lemon meringue pie and coffee touched slightly on the truth. She had thrown her cape over Luke because she had seen the symptoms of shock, had rushed to call 911, stayed behind to clarify things for the authorities while I had left. And neither of us had seen Virginia or any sign of life, for that matter. Just the poor dead girl, so obviously dead that she, Mary Alice, hadn't touched her because she wouldn't want to contaminate a crime scene.

"Good thinking," Virgil said.

"Hand me one of those little milk things," I told Sister. "A couple of them."

I waited until she had them in the air. "We didn't even know it was a snake-handling church."

Nondairy creamer squirted all over the table.

"Damn!" Sister hopped up and grabbed my sleeve. "Excuse us a minute, Virgil."

"What the hell do you mean, a snake-handling church?" she demanded as soon as she closed the restroom door. "We were in there with snakes?"

"That's what that box was for up at the front. The woman in the ambulance told me. She says they get called up there sometimes when folks get bitten."

Sister looked pale. I was beginning to feel a little guilty. So she had altered the version of the role she had played at the church. Who would want to admit they had been upchucking all over the parking lot? Especially to a man you were obviously attracted to.

"I'm sorry. I thought you knew," I lied.

"Biggest rattlesnakes in the world on the mountains around here." A voice from a stall. The toilet flushed and a plump, very blond

64

woman stepped out, buttoning her pants. She turned on the water and soaped her hands. "Lots of folks like to play with them. They're not slimy like you think they'd be."

Neither of us said anything.

"Y'all have a good evening now." She dried her hands on a paper towel and left.

"What the hell was Virginia thinking of? A snake handler?" Sister opened her purse, took out a comb, and began to comb her hair, looking at it from several angles. She hadn't had it colored since before we went to Warsaw and it was turning slightly orange.

"Maybe she was looking for excitement."

"Sounds like she found it. I wonder if Luke knows."

"I doubt it."

Another woman came into the restroom. "How y'all doing?"

"Fine," we said together.

"We'd better get back," Sister said. "He's nice, isn't he?"

"Married?"

"Widowed. Two years."

We left the restroom and headed back toward the table.

"Graduate of Annapolis, retired from the navy after twenty years, sheriff for fifteen, three grown children."

I learned all this between the bathroom and the table. But when had *she* learned it?

Virgil Stuckey hopped up as we approached.

"I'm sorry," Mary Alice said, sliding into a chair. "I had no idea that was a snake-handling church."

Virgil smiled. "I figured as much, the way the milk went flying."

He motioned for the waitress to bring us some more coffee.

"You okay?" he asked Sister.

"Patricia Anne just startled me."

Virgil frowned at me. I should be ashamed startling this delicate creature in the purple boots.

"Actually," he said, "that's one of the most active snake-handling churches in north Alabama. And Monk Crawford is one of the best known of the snake-handling preachers."

"Have mercy." Sister fanned herself with a paper napkin and turned to me. "I don't remember Virginia liking snakes, do you?" And then to Virgil, "Virginia's a Lutheran."

We were quiet while the waitress poured our coffee.

"Her son's in the House of Representatives and she belongs to the country club, doesn't she, Patricia Anne? Plays golf."

I nodded. "Do you know who the dead girl is?" I asked Virgil.

"We have an idea. We should know for sure tomorrow."

"There was red clay on her boots. The ground around the church is sandy."

"Oh, for heaven's sake, y'all," Sister said. "Let's talk about something else. Snake handling and dead people. Lord. Do you like to dance, Virgil?"

Virgil allowed as to how he did.

Sister grinned at me.

I got up.

66

"Where are you going?" she asked.

"To see if 'Unchained Melody' is on the jukebox."

It wasn't, but "These Boots Are Made for Walkin' " was. I figured that was apropos.

By the time we drove back to Birmingham the snow had turned into a fine mist. The temperature was probably thirty-three degrees, so close to freezing that the moisture hitting the windshield seemed oily.

Sister was unusually quiet.

"The sheriff seems nice," I said.

"Hmmm," was her reply.

"Do you think Virginia was in the church?"

"Don't know."

End of conversation. I closed my eyes and listened to Pachelbel's Canon in D that radio station WBHM was playing. So much had happened and I was so keyed up, I had no idea that I would go to sleep. But I did. In fact, I was shopping in Warsaw with Haley when the car stopped and Sister said, "You're home, and your mouth's open."

True enough. I closed my mouth, told her I would talk to her in the morning, and stepped from the car into a curtain of mist. Fred had left the back light on and the deck off the kitchen looked icy. Typical Birmingham January, I thought. Warm one day, freezing the next.

Fred opened the back door for me, leaned forward and held out his hand.

"Be careful. That porch is slippery."

"I thought you'd be in bed," I said, taking his hand and stepping into the warm kitchen.

"Couldn't sleep until you got in."

Chances were he'd already had three hours sleep in his recliner, but that was okay.

"How's Luke?"

"About the same." I had called from Oneonta and told Fred about Luke's concussion. "They're just keeping him for observation."

Fred was hugging me, his arms inside my coat. He had on his old velour robe that smelled like Gain soap. I rubbed my cheek against it and considered going to sleep standing up.

"I've got to go to bed," I said. "I'm beat."

Fred followed me down the hall. "No sign of Virginia?"

"Nope." I sat on the edge of the bed and kicked my shoes off. "The guy she ran off with is a snake handler, though."

"What?"

"He's a snake-handling preacher." I pointed toward the bathroom door. "Hand me my nightgown and robe."

"I thought he was a painter."

"He is." I started shucking clothes.

"How did you find that out?" Fred held out my gown and flannel robe.

"The woman in the ambulance told me. And the sheriff says he's one of the best-known ones in north Alabama."

"What sheriff?"

"Virgil Stuckey. The sheriff of St. Clair County. There was a body in the church and I think Sister's smitten with him, the sheriff. They both seem smitten."

"What do you mean, a body?"

"A woman's body."

My nightgown was on.

"I'll tell you in the morning," I said. And for what was probably the first time in sixty years, I went to sleep without washing my face and brushing my teeth and with my clothes in a pile by the bed. Jet lag is a killer.

Needless to say, I had a lot to explain to Fred in the morning. I woke up when I heard him in the shower and felt surprisingly rested. The sun was shining and there was no sign of the flurries of the night before. I brushed my teeth, combed my hair, and had French toast ready to cook when he came into the kitchen.

"A body?" Not even a "good morning."

Two pieces of French toast and a couple of cups of coffee later, I had told him the main parts of the story.

"And Virginia and the preacher were gone? Her car wasn't there?"

I hadn't thought about Virginia's car. I guess I had assumed that since she was the runee, she had left in the runner's vehicle. Or was she the runner? At any rate, of course she would have taken her car and followed Holden Crawford. Monk Crawford.

"It wasn't there," I said. "Only his painting truck."

"Sounds like she's got herself in a mess."

"God's truth," I agreed.

"You don't think the dead woman could have been this Crawford guy's wife, do you?"

"Too young. Bless her heart." I could see the red hair cascading to the floor.

"Well, don't you and Mary Alice get mixed up in this, honey. You stay away from those folks."

"You don't have a thing to worry about. I can't even watch the Discovery Channel specials about snakes."

He gave me a hug. "Call me when you get home with Luke." He got a Lean Cuisine from the freezer for his lunch and left. That was when I turned on the computer and read Haley's chatty E-mail.

The phone was ringing when I got out of the shower. I figured it would be Mary Alice so I was startled when a male voice said, "Mrs. Hollowell? This is Sheriff Stuckey."

"Good morning, Sheriff." Hmm. Last night it had been Virgil and Patricia Anne.

"I'm calling you because I didn't want to disturb Mary Alice."

"She does need her beauty sleep," Mrs. Hollowell said.

"Not that I can see."

How does Sister do this to men?

"But, Mrs. Hollowell, we've had something come up. Your cousin's car has been found in Pulaski, Tennessee."

"Virginia's car?"

"Right. Mrs. Nelson's. The license tag checks out to Mr. Nelson, but her stuff is in the glove compartment so we figured it was her car. Can you tell me what model car she drove?"

"Lord, no. A car's a car to me. I can't even find my own Chevrolet in a parking lot. Why? Was the car abandoned?"

"Some hunters found it early this morning in the woods near Pulaski."

"Wrecked?"

"Not exactly."

He was being too cagey.

"But?"

There was a long pause. I could tell he was trying to decide whether to tell me something or not.

"Monk Crawford's body was in it."

"Oh, my Lord." I sat down on the bed. "What happened? And what about Virginia?"

"We don't know. We don't know any of the details. All the Pulaski authorities said was that the car and body had been found. There was identification on the body and they want us to notify Monk's family. We're trying to locate them now."

I rubbed my forehead; my head was beginning to ache.

"And no sign of Virginia?"

"No."

Again there was that hesitancy in his voice, but I knew.

"Monk was killed, wasn't he? Murdered?"

Virgil Stuckey cleared his throat. "Like I said, Mrs. Hollowell, we don't know the details, but the Pulaski police think that he was. Yes."

In Virginia's car.

"What I was thinking," he continued, "was that Mrs. Nelson's family should be told what's happened, too."

I couldn't argue with that. Virginia had run off with a man who had turned out to be a snake-handling preacher, a young woman had been murdered in his church, Luke had possibly been attacked in that same church, and now the preacher had been found dead, murdered. In Virginia's car.

"I'll call her son," I said. "He's in Washington. He's the representative from Columbus, Mississippi. His father should have called him when this first happened."

"And Mr. Nelson?"

"I'm going to Oneonta. They're supposed to release him this afternoon. I'll tell him."

"If we learn anything else in the meantime, I'll call you."

After I thanked him and hung up the phone, I went into the den, found my address book and took it into the kitchen where the sun was shining brightly through the bay window and where Muffin was sitting on the kitchen table, grooming herself. When I put on my reading glasses, I could see cat hair like motes floating in the sunlight. And I'm the one who has always complained about Mary Alice's old cat, Bubba, who sleeps on a heating pad on her kitchen counter.

I sat down at the table and opened my address book. It's the same one that half the women in the United States own, the one from the Metropolitan Museum of Art with the painting by Mary Cassatt on the cover of a woman licking an envelope. I'm convinced that if I lost it, my whole social life, such as it is, would fall apart.

I opened it to the *N*s. There was Luke and Virginia's address and phone number in Columbus. But no address or phone number for Richard. If I knew how to use the Internet well enough, I could have found him in a minute. But the class I'd signed up for at UAB didn't start for a couple of weeks. Well, I thought, it shouldn't be too hard to find someone in the House of Representatives.

But what on God's earth was I going to tell him?

I propped my elbows on the table and put my face in my hands. Muffin came to rub against my hair.

I'd never been very fond of Virginia, granted, but it was sad and frightening to think of what might have happened to her. Whatever her problems had been with Luke, however depressed and desperate she might have been, she had jumped from the frying pan into the fire.

I raised my head. Muffin's eyes looked right into mine. I pulled her against me and buried my face in her fur. She smelled like sweet, healthy cat; she began to purr. Lord, was I going to be able to let Haley take her back?

There was a light knock on the back door. I got up and let Mitzi Phizer in. My neighbor and friend for almost forty years, she knows me too well.

"Lord, Patricia Anne. What's wrong?"

She's also a wonderful listener. Except for a few "I declares" and "Have mercies," she didn't interrupt my story about all that had happened in the last twenty-four hours.

When I finally wound down, she said, "You think Virginia's dead, too, don't you?"

"I think it's a good possibility, and it makes me so sad. I can't imagine how she must have felt when she found out what she had gotten into, can you?"

Mitzi shook her head no.

"And it's more than the snakes. There's something going on up there that two people have been murdered over." I paused. "Surely there's some connection between the two deaths."

"I would think so."

"And now I've got to call Richard and tell him what's happened, and I dread it. To start with, it's not going to make any sense to him. He's going to think I've lost my mind when I tell him his mother ran off with a snake-handling preacher."

"Why don't you get Mary Alice to call him?"

I looked up and Mitzi was smiling at me.

"I'll take Woofer for his walk. You go tell her what's happened. Tell her the sheriff suggested the call."

I thought of the sheriff not wanting to disturb Miss Purple Boots's beauty sleep.

I smiled back. "That's a great idea."

Mary Alice lives in a house on top of Red Mountain, a huge house that her first husband Will Alec Sullivan's family built with the millions they made off of steel. Her other two wealthy husbands had been happy to live with her there; each, like his predecessor, had impregnated her once there, and had widowed her there. They would have been crazy not to have lived there. It's one of the most beautiful houses I've ever seen, overlooking the whole city. From Sister's sunroom, you can see planes landing and taking off from the airport. You can see thunderstorms roaring down the valley, and spectacular sunsets.

This morning as I pulled into the driveway, Tiffany the Magic Maid was sweeping the front porch. She is a cute young blonde. The Magic Maids is the name of the company that she works for though, best I can tell, she spends most of her time at Mary Alice's.

She looked up and waved. It was all of thirty-five degrees but she had on khaki shorts and a blue denim shirt. Her arms and legs were as tan as if it were July.

"Morning, Mrs. Hollowell," she called.

"Morning, Tiffany. Did you see the snow last night?"

"Sure did. Wasn't it pretty?"

"And cold."

She giggled. "I'm just going to stay out here a minute. Mrs. Crane's in the sunroom eating breakfast."

I let myself into the house and walked back to the sunroom where Mary Alice was reading the paper and drinking coffee.

"Hey," she said, pointing toward a white carafe. "You want a cup? There's some toast left, too."

"Nope." I sat down in one of the white wicker chairs that's covered in a bright floral print. Next to my kitchen this is my favorite room in the whole world.

Sister folded the paper and put it on the coffee table.

"What's up? You're out early. Is Luke okay?"

"I guess so. I haven't heard. Virgil Stuckey called, though."

Sister came to attention. Preened, actually. "Really?" She smoothed the silky yellow caftan she was wearing. "What did he want?"

I told her. It didn't take as long as it had taken me to tell Mitzi because it was just the part about the car in Pulaski, Monk Crawford's body, and our need to call Richard. I did get a "Well, I do declare," out of her, though.

"And there's no sign of Virginia?"

"Well, Luke said he saw her in the church, remember."

"I don't think he did. I'll bet she's dead."

Sister got up, brushing toast crumbs from the yellow silk.

"Say Virgil thought we ought to call Richard?"

I nodded.

"Do you know his number?"

"No."

"Well, it shouldn't be too hard to find."

She went into the kitchen and came back with a phone and a phone book.

"I'll just call our representative's office here. They'll have a directory of all the congressmen."

And they did. Sister wrote down Richard's number and dialed it. Apparently his secretary answered and asked if she wanted

Richard's voice mail when Sister identified herself.

When Richard got back to his office he was greeted with a message that went like this:

> *Richard, this is your cousin, Mary Alice Crane from Birmingham. Right after Christmas your mama ran off with a man named Holden Crawford who's a snake-handling preacher up on Chandler Mountain and whose body has been found in your mother's car in Pulaski, Tennessee. And your daddy's in the Blount County Medical Center with a bad concussion, though they think he'll be all right if his brain doesn't swell. He probably just fell and hit his head on a bench when he saw the woman's body in the church. We don't know where your mama is, but you might want to give us a call.*

"Okay," Sister said, putting the phone down. "That ought to do it."

Chapter Seven

"Do what?"

Eight-and-a-half-months pregnant, Debbie Lamont was standing in the doorway, filling the doorway. I've never understood this glow that pregnant women are supposed to have. I know I never had it. Maybe they're talking about those few hormonal days when you feel flushed, the days between the green of nausea and the gray of weariness. Debbie was definitely at the gray stage.

"Come sit down, sweetheart," her mother said. "You wouldn't believe all that's happened."

Debbie gave her mother a kiss, blew me one, and eased herself down sideways on the sofa.

"Morning, Aunt Pat. Henry made Uncle Fred that beef-tip-and-rice casserole he likes so much. I took it by your house and saw Mrs. Phizer walking Woofer. She said you were here."

"Thank you, darling. And thank Henry. Fred will think he's died and gone to heaven."

"I put it in the refrigerator." Debbie looked over at her mother. "What ought to do it?"

"What?"

"You said 'That ought to do it.' "

"It's a long story. Your Aunt Pat will tell you. You want some coffee?"

"Decaf?"

"Sure." Sister started toward the kitchen. "Tell her what's happened, Mouse."

So for the third time that morning I had to relate the saga of Luke, Virginia, and Holden Crawford. The late Holden Crawford. Debbie was by far the best audience I had had.

She clutched her chest. "Oh, my Lord, Aunt Pat. That's awful. Poor Virginia. Poor Luke."

"Well, it's not all awful." Sister handed

Debbie her coffee. "Tell her about the sheriff, Mouse."

"His name is Virgil Stuckey. He liked your mother's purple boots."

"He looks like Cary Grant, Debbie."

I am a kind person. I wasn't about to mention the fact that he was a dead ringer for Willard Scott and General Schwarzkopf.

"Well, what does this Virgil Stuckey say about what's going on?"

"He said he thought it was time to alert Richard in Washington," I explained. "Which your mother just did. She left him a message."

"Just told him about the bodies and his mother being missing and his daddy hurt."

Debbie smiled. "You're right. That ought to do it, Mama."

She sipped her coffee and tried to get comfortable. "I don't think this baby is going to wait two more weeks. Can y'all see the way he's knotted up on the side?"

That reminded me. I reached in my purse and handed Debbie the velvet bag that I had planned to take by her house the day before.

"A present from Philip."

She put her coffee down and grinned. "Jewelry?"

"The family jewels."

The look on her face was priceless when she pulled the neutercal from the bag.

"Oooh, what is this?" She held the prosthetic testicle in her hand. "It squishes and there's something hard in it."

"Let me see that." Sister took the neutercal

from Debbie. "Hey, this is a really great fake nut."

"It's called a neutercal," I explained to Debbie. "You squeeze it when you're in labor. Philip says the doctors in Warsaw swear it cuts labor time in half."

"Give it here, Mama." Debbie snatched the neutercal back, gave it a good squeeze, and laughed. "This is wonderful." She squeezed again. "Oh, my, yes. I can see how this would work wonders."

"Let me try it," Sister said.

Debbie handed it over reluctantly. We were giggling when Tiffany came in. She had to have a squeeze, too, declaring it was just a fancy stress ball like Alabama midwives used all the time.

"Nowadays?" Debbie asked.

"I'm sure they do, cause they work. My grandmama was a midwife. She'd get everybody to save those little cotton tobacco pouches with the drawstring tops for her. You know, the ones for people who rolled their own cigarettes? She'd fill them up with grits. Put a marble in them." Tiffany handed the neutercal back to Debbie. "Said it worked wonders."

"I never heard of them," Sister said.

Tiffany shrugged, a "city folks don't know much" shrug.

She was right. There was a lot we city folks didn't know. About snake handling, for instance.

"Where did you grow up, Tiffany?" I asked.

"Tuscaloosa. My daddy teaches chemistry

at the university. But my grandmama who was the midwife lived near Sterrett. She and my grandpa had a farm, raised peaches mostly. Why?"

"I don't suppose they ever ran into any snake handlers."

"What?"

This time it was Sister who told the story. When she finished, Tiffany declared, "I can't believe that. Poor soul."

I wasn't sure whether she meant the red-headed girl, Monk Crawford, or Virginia. I guess it didn't matter.

"Somebody help me up," Debbie said. "I have to go to the bathroom."

"She got that ball just in time," Tiffany said watching Debbie waddle through the door. Then, "What are y'all going to do? Wait for the sheriff to call or go on up to Oneonta?"

"I think we should go on up there and tell Luke," Sister said. "I'll put the phone on call forwarding in case Richard calls. And we can stop by the sheriff's office and see if he's heard anything."

"Wear your purple boots," I suggested.

Sister giggled.

Luke looked worse than he had the night before. Both eyes were black and he groaned when he saw us.

"I'm seeing two of you."

"There are two of us," Mary Alice said.

"No. I mean I'm seeing four of you. Two each."

"Is that normal when you have a concussion?"

Luke looked at the two Mary Alices and said, "Hell, no, it's not normal. I think my eyes got jarred out of their sockets."

Sister sat down in the only chair and examined Luke's eyes. "They look like they're fitting okay. Not a good color, but straight."

"What did the doctor say?" Luke's appearance was alarming. I wondered if the double vision was a sign of the swelling they had warned us about.

"They're going to do a CAT scan or an MRI or something in a little while. One of those alphabet things where they stick you in a tube."

"They'll just stick your head in," Mary Alice assured him. "The rest of you is working, isn't it?"

"I reckon. All I've had to eat is a banana popsicle."

"I love banana popsicles. Don't you, Mouse?"

I agreed that I did.

"And lime and grape." Sister leaned forward. "Luke, there's something we have to tell you."

Something he was in no condition to hear. But Sister surprised me.

"After they do the CAT scan and let you go, we're going to take you to my house. In my Jaguar."

Luke smiled and clasped Mary Alice's hand. Just at that moment the door opened and two orderlies came in with a gurney.

82

"Gotta take you down to radiology, Mr. Nelson."

He was still smiling when he was wheeled out.

"That was nice," I told Sister.

"Well, did you get a good look at him? There's no way on God's earth they're going to let that man out today. Come on. Let's go down to Joe's and get some lunch."

Which is where both Richard and Virgil Stuckey located us. Virgil first, fortunately. We had just sat down when he came walking into the restaurant. This did not surprise me. Nor Sister. She smiled and waved.

My back was to the door. "Cary Grant?" I ventured.

"You got it."

"I was hoping I would catch you here," the sheriff said.

Mary Alice motioned toward a chair. He pulled it out quickly and sat down.

"You ladies okay?"

We assured him that we were.

"Fixing to order lunch," Sister said. "Why don't you join us?"

As if he weren't already sitting down.

"Fine. Thanks. How's your cousin?"

"Seeing double. They're doing some more tests." Sister handed him a menu that was stuck between the salt and pepper and a bottle of pepper sauce. "Have you found out anything else?"

"We've identified the woman in the church. Monk Crawford's daughter-in-law named Susan. Married to his son Ethan who died last year from a rattlesnake he was handling. They say it hung on and wouldn't let go, emptied so much venom in him they couldn't save him. His arm swelled up big as an elephant's leg. Turned black."

A waitress came up to take our order. The vegetable plate had looked good a few minutes before. Now I decided iced tea was all I wanted. Surprisingly, it was all Sister ordered, too. I glanced over at her. Definitely pale.

"What's the matter?" Virgil asked. "I didn't take your appetite away, did I?"

"A little bit," Sister confessed, surprising me again.

"Well, I'm so sorry." And to the waitress, "I'll just have iced tea, too."

"No, you go on and eat," Sister said. "It's fine."

"You're sure?'

We nodded.

He ordered practically everything on the menu. "I've got to head out for Pulaski in a little while, and I don't know when I'll get a chance to eat again."

"Tell us about Susan Crawford," I said.

He looked at Mary Alice for permission. She nodded.

"She was a handler, too. Big time. She and her husband used to go all over the mountains up here and even Georgia and Tennessee holding meetings, testifying, and handling."

"Was she still doing it?" I asked.

"Far as I can tell. She had a couple of kids, though, little ones, so I guess after her husband died she didn't have as much opportunity."

And now those children were orphaned. Their father and mother were dead and so was their grandfather.

"Where are the children now?" Sister asked.

"We're not sure."

"I don't understand any of this," I said. And I didn't. I couldn't imagine the religious fervor, the letting go of one's self that would allow someone to handle serpents to prove his faith.

"They claim they're in a state of ecstasy while they're handling and talking in tongues," Virgil said.

No, I couldn't understand it. But neither could I judge it. The passion that had twisted Susan Crawford's neck all the way around, however, was a different matter.

"Do you know yet what happened to Monk Crawford?" I asked.

"Nope." He was lying; his ears turned red.

"Oh, that must be Richard." Sister reached in her purse and handed me a vibrating phone. "Answer it, Patricia Anne."

"How?"

She mashed a button. "Just say hello."

"Hello?"

"Mary Alice?"

"Just a minute." I handed the phone back to Sister. "He wants to talk to you."

Virgil Stuckey was looking from one of us to the other.

Sister gave in. "I'd better take this in the bathroom." As she got up she narrowly missed colliding with the waitress who was bringing Virgil's lunch. "Sorry."

Virgil watched her walk away from the table. She might not be wearing the purple boots today, but she was still creating a gleam in his eye.

The waitress put the food down and Virgil sprinkled pepper sauce on his turnip greens.

"What happened to Monk Crawford's wife?" I asked him.

"Something normal, I understand. Something like pneumonia." He buttered a piece of cornbread. "Tell me about Virginia Nelson, other than she played golf and belonged to the country club."

I admitted that I really didn't know her that well. "She must have been desperately unhappy, though, to leave like she did."

"She and her husband get along?"

"We thought they did. We just see them at weddings and things, though." I hesitated. "They tend to drink a little too much on those occasions. I don't know what it's like at home, the alcohol." I paused and watched Virgil inhale a whole new potato. "I do know that Luke was truly devastated when he got to my house. I think it's the last thing in the world he thought would happen."

"They just have the one child?"

I nodded. "Richard. The representative."

I sipped my tea and wondered how Richard was taking the news that Mary Alice was passing along. I wondered how much she was telling him.

The restaurant was filling up with the

lunch crowd. Several people spoke to the sheriff as they walked by. He called most of them by name, I noticed. I remarked on this.

"I used to know just about everybody in this county and my county, too," he said. "Then half the folks from Birmingham decided to move out here." He inhaled another potato. "I can't say I blame them. It's beautiful out here. Getting sort of crowded though. I worry about the animals, the deer and the foxes."

A man after my own heart.

"Even the Chandler Mountain booger?"

He grinned. "Especially the booger."

Sister sat back down. "Richard's getting the first flight that he can. He'll probably be in early this evening. He said not to meet him, that he'd rent a car."

Neither of us asked how he had taken the news.

Sister eyed the food that was left in front of Virgil Stuckey.

"That looks good."

Virgil nodded. "Is."

"Patricia Anne, maybe we ought to order something. We need to keep our strength up."

It was close to an hour before we got back to the hospital. Telling Virgil goodbye took quite a while. He promised to call if there was any news of Virginia. In fact, he would just call anyway. And chances were he'd be back the next day. The sheriff was a smitten man.

"He's too young for you," I said to Sister who was doing a little skipping step down the sidewalk. "He's not twenty-eight years older."

"I know. Isn't it wonderful? I might not have to bury this one."

"How many plots do you have left at Elmwood?"

"Just two. And one of those is for me. He might want to be buried with his first wife anyway. Though I doubt it."

Amazing. There was Sheriff Virgil Stuckey driving up the road to Pulaski, Tennessee, with no idea in the world that my sister already had him hog-tied for eternity. A man she had met just the day before.

"Aren't you still engaged to Cedric?" I asked.

"Who?"

"The Englishman."

"I don't think so."

Luke was spooning tapioca pudding from a plastic cup when we got back.

"They're not going to let me leave," he said mournfully.

"Oh, Luke, I'm so sorry." Mary Alice actually patted his foot which was sticking out from under the sheet. The woman has no conscience. "What did they say?"

"Maybe tomorrow." He blinked back tears. "And I'm so worried about Virginia. I know she's up there at that church, not knowing I'm hurt."

"She's fine, Luke," I said. "She's going to show up soon."

"Of course she is," Sister agreed. "And we'll come back to get you tomorrow. Okay?"

"In the Jaguar?"

"Absolutely."

The poor fellow smiled. I could have kicked Sister in the butt, especially when we were walking down the hall and she said, "Did you see Luke's toenails? Longer than Howard Hughes's. If he cut them he'd wear a size smaller shoe, I swear."

It was my idea to go back over Chandler Mountain and go home the way we had come the day before. I knew we weren't going to find Virginia at the church, and that I, for one, wouldn't set foot in that church with that box at the front even if the police didn't have it cordoned off, which they probably did. But I wanted to see it, knowing what I did know about all that had happened there.

So we wound up the steep curves that I had traveled down in the ambulance the day before. The view over the edge made me appreciate again how carefully the ambulance driver had taken the curves. One mistake and we'd have been in the next county or in the heavenly choir.

The weather had done a complete turnaround in twenty-four hours. It was in the midfifties with bright sun striping the road through bare branches of trees, trees that clung to the rocky bank over the road and threatened to crash down at any minute. We didn't meet another car all the way up the mountain.

The Jesus Is Our Life and Heaven Hereafter church was built on the bluff side and was, since the road ran so close to the bluff, the first building on that side of the road. I hadn't realized the day before that the back of the church would have been jutting over a deep ravine if it weren't for a large rock formation.

There was no crime tape across the front of the church, and the only vehicle in sight was Holden Crawford's paint van.

Mary Alice pulled into the driveway between the house and church and stopped.

"They don't have much parking space here, do they?"

"No. Looks like they park in front of the house. The yard's all rutted."

Then she voiced what I was thinking. "I wonder what Virginia thought when she first saw this place."

"That she was in over her head, I imagine, especially when she found out what was going on over at the church."

"But she didn't leave."

"Maybe she couldn't."

Mary Alice tapped her nails against the steering wheel. "I wonder if the police checked the back of the van."

"I'm sure they did. Virginia's missing and her car is found in Tennessee with Monk Crawford's body in it. They checked all right." I looked toward the church. "But, you know, a person could fall off one of those rocks and never be found unless they happened to get caught in a tree."

"You're thinking Monk Crawford killed her and went to Tennessee in her car?"

"Well, I don't know," I admitted. "He wouldn't have brought her up here just for her car."

90

"And she was nobody's Pamela Anderson."

"Who?"

"*Baywatch*. Boobs."

"No. She was a sixty-something-year-old woman. Doesn't make sense."

"Money?"

"You think she had any?"

"Probably some."

"Well, that should be fairly easy to check out."

The sound of wheels on gravel made us turn around. A red pickup truck had pulled into the driveway behind us. I was relieved to see a nice-looking young couple in their late twenties get out. The woman, I realized instantly, had to be Susan Crawford's sister. The same red hair fell almost to her waist; she was carrying a pot of pink hydrangeas wrapped in pink foil. They walked up to my side of the car, and I let the window down.

"Afternoon," the girl said. "I'm Betsy Mahall and this is my husband, Terry. Can we help you with something?"

"We just stopped for a minute," I explained, introducing Mary Alice and myself. "We were here yesterday."

"The ladies who found Susan?" Terry Mahall was very tall and thin, at least a foot taller than his wife. He put his arm protectively around her shoulders. "She was Betsy's sister."

"I'm so sorry."

Betsy Mahall nodded. "I brought these flowers to put in the church." Her eyes welled with tears. "I guess it doesn't matter, but I wanted to."

"Of course it matters, honey," Terry Mahall said. "Here, let me hold those for you."

Betsy surrendered the hydrangeas and fished in her jacket pocket for a Kleenex.

"I'm sorry," she said, holding the Kleenex to her eyes. "I don't guess I've stopped crying since I got the word yesterday. And then when we heard about Monk this morning—"

"Why don't you sit in the car a minute?" Mary Alice offered.

"Why don't you do that, honey? You've just about made yourself sick." Terry Mahall opened the back door for his wife. "I'll go put these in the church."

Betsy hesitated. "Y'all sure you don't need to leave?"

We assured her that we weren't in a hurry.

"Thanks." She climbed into the car and sank down on the seat with a sigh. "I don't think I've ever been so tired in my life."

We watched Terry cross to the church.

Betsy shivered. "I hope the door's not locked."

"It wasn't yesterday." Sister turned and looked at the girl. "You want some aspirin? And I've got some coffee up here in a thermos."

Betsy shook her head. "My ears are already ringing I've had so much aspirin. But I'd like for you to tell me about yesterday. About Susan." She paused. "If you don't mind."

"You tell her," Sister said.

Terry disappeared into the church with the hydrangeas. I wondered if he would put them on the box at the front. I assumed he knew what the box usually held.

"My cousin was looking for his wife," I explained. "He went into the church and didn't come back out, and we went in to see about him. He had fallen and was unconscious and Susan was lying on the front bench." I decided not to add any details.

"Did she look peaceful?" Betsy asked.

"She looked dead." Mary Alice realized how blunt this sounded and tried to soften it. "But neat in spite of her neck."

"It was like someone had laid her out," I explained, frowning at Sister.

Betsy sighed. "I always thought it would be the snakes that took her. I thought her husband Ethan's dying from snakebite would put some sense in her, but it did just the opposite. She said she had to do his work, too."

"You're not a handler, then?"

"Lord, no. Susan took it up when she married Ethan. She even kept those things under her bed, but I wouldn't let her come near my house with them. I'm scared to death of snakes."

"You and me both," Mary Alice agreed.

"What about her children?" I asked. "Weren't they in danger?"

"Oh, no, ma'am. Susan and Ethan both adored those babies. They were careful."

I wondered how careful you could be with poisonous snakes under your bed and toddlers roaming around.

"How old are the children?" I asked.

"Jamie's four and Ethan Jr.'s two. Bless their hearts." Betsy wiped her eyes again. "I was keeping them while Susan was in Georgia.

I didn't even know she was back until the sheriff called. She wasn't supposed to be back until today." She paused. "And then he called again this morning about Monk. I swear, my head's just spinning."

Mary Alice held up the thermos. "Sure you don't want some?"

"No, ma'am. But thanks. You know, I think I'll go in the church and pray a little." She opened the door and hesitated. "There's not anything in there, is it?"

"In the church?" I asked. "You mean like snakes? I don't think so."

"Or blood?"

"If there is, it's our cousin's."

"Oh, okay."

Betsy started toward the church and then turned and came back to the car. I let the window down again.

"I wish you could have seen how beautiful Susan was," she said.

"We did."

She nodded, turned, and walked toward her husband who had come out of the church.

"That's just downright pitiful," Sister said. "That poor girl."

I agreed.

"You still want to go look over the bluff and see if we see Virginia caught in a tree?"

I thought not.

Chapter Eight

FROM: HALEY
TO: MAMA AND PAPA
SUBJECT: POLISH COOKING

Mama, you're not going to believe this. I signed up for a cooking class, figured I'd come home with some fancy Polish dishes that would impress even Henry. So I showed up, with my English-Polish dictionary, of course, so I could look up the exotic ingredients.

Anyway, there were twelve people in the class, ten women and two men, and a couple of them spoke enough English so I didn't feel totally at a loss.

So in comes the chef, a very well-fed man with a huge chef's hat. I was impressed. He announced what we were going to cook, and one of the ladies who spoke English told me "chicken." They all seemed very excited. So was I until he got out a huge skillet into which he dumped almost a whole can of Crisco, dipped the chicken pieces into egg and then flour, and proceeded to fry them. Southern fried chicken, Mama! Polish soul food. I admit it tasted wonderful, though.

Hugs and greasy kisses,
Haley

The phone rang as soon as I turned off the computer.

DEBBIE: We're on our way to the hospital, Aunt Pat. Y'all come on down. Henry wants you to see him bring David Anthony out to weigh him and put his little cap and diaper on.

ME: Wake up, Fred. Debbie and Henry are on their way to the hospital. We've got to go see David Anthony as soon as he's born.

FRED: What time is it?

ME: Eight o'clock.

FRED: At night?

Maybe we weren't over the jet lag as much as I had thought.

Henry Lamont is one of the special people in my life. If I had had to bet on one of my students becoming a famous writer, it would have been Henry. He still may get around to it some day. Or maybe he won't, which is fine. He's a wonderful, creative chef, a job that he loves and that all of us enjoy. I couldn't have been more pleased when he became part of our family.

Mrs. Lamont, we were informed when we got to the hospital, was in one of the birthing rooms on the fourth floor. Just inquire at the desk up there.

"Birthing room?" Fred asked as we got on

96

the elevator. "Is that the same as a delivery room?"

"Not quite," I explained. "It's like a very nice bedroom and the whole family can stay in there with the mother while she's in labor and while the baby's being born."

"What?" The elevator door closed, but Fred didn't punch the button.

I reached over and hit four. "Sure. We're the cheerleaders." I waved an imaginary pompom. "Push, Debbie, push!"

"Not funny, Patricia Anne."

"I know, sweetheart." I put both arms around his waist. "But don't you wish you could have been with me when our children were born? That you had been the one to hand them to me while they were still attached to the umbilical cord?"

"Lord, no. Will Henry have to do that?"

"Henry *wants* to do that. He wants to bond immediately with David Anthony."

"Well, that's fine, I guess. He'd still better send Debbie some flowers, though."

The door opened and we stepped out.

"I sent you roses every time."

"There's one pressed in each of their baby books." I took his hand. "You want to have another one?"

"I think I'll pass." He grinned. "But thanks for the offer."

"Hey, Aunt Pat. Uncle Fred." Henry was walking down the hall. He held up a Styrofoam cup. "I just came out to get some coffee. Y'all come on back. Debbie's in birthing room two."

"How's she doing?" I asked.

"Great. The doctor says he doesn't think it'll be long. Mary Alice is already here."

"Maybe I'd better wait out here." Fred pointed to a room where several people sat watching a TV bolted high on a side wall. Below the TV was a large window with a closed Venetian blind.

"Well, come on speak to Debbie first." Henry pointed to the waiting room. "I'll bring David Anthony to the room next door as soon as Debbie's held him and loved him some. They'll open the blinds and you can see them weighing him and putting the drops in his eyes."

I squeezed Fred's hand. I had seen Haley bring the twins, Fay and May, out when they were born. But Fred had been out of town. He had no idea what a thrill he was in for.

Walking into the birthing room was like walking into a posh bed and breakfast run by Laura Ashley. Except for a few discreet monitors and beeping sounds and the fact that Debbie was squeezing on the neutercal and told Henry to go to hell, this could have been any romantic hideaway.

"Okay, sweetheart," he said. "Your Aunt Pat and Uncle Fred are here. You want some more ice?"

"No. Hey, y'all."

I went over and kissed her; Fred waved from the doorway.

"Where's your mama?" I asked.

"Out in the hall or somewhere talking to that Virgil guy. I'm on the verge of having this baby

98

and Henry's out getting snacks and Mama's sweet-talking some man."

"I'm here, honey." Henry smoothed her hair back from her forehead. "I won't leave again."

Tears oozed from the corners of Debbie's eyes.

"I'm acting horrible, Aunt Pat. Did I act this bad when the girls were born?"

"Sure you did," I assured her.

A woman dressed in a delicately flowered Laura Ashley granny dress brushed by Fred who was still standing by the door. She smiled at all of us, checked the monitors, said, "Doing fine. Love that stress ball," and left.

Damn. A delivery theme park.

Debbie groaned and squeezed the neutercal.

"Honey," Fred said, backing out of the room. "Your Aunt Pat and I are going to wait down the hall. Okay?"

"Okay. I'm really not hurting much, though. I just feel these urges."

Urges? That was when Fred disappeared. I was about to follow him when Mary Alice walked in.

"Did you see those heavy Birkenstock sandals that nurse was wearing with that cute Laura Ashley dress? Ruined the whole effect. Hey, Mouse. I saw Fred skedadlling down the hall."

"Hey. How's Virgil?"

"Fine. He's found out some stuff. I'll tell you later."

"Has he found Virginia?"

"Maybe."

"I want some ice," Debbie said.

In a few minutes I joined Fred in the waiting room where he was watching a basketball game on TV.

"Who's playing?" I asked.

"I'm not sure. The ones in the blue are winning."

I sat down beside him and took his hand.

One of the Laura nurses stuck her head in the doorway. "Caldwells? Your baby's on her way."

Four people jumped up and rushed to the window. The venetian blind opened and they oohed and aahed, laughed and cried.

"Let's look," I told Fred.

We joined them at the window. Two nurses, dressed in green scrubs (reassuring) were ministering to a purplish-red baby who was not at all happy about what had just happened to her. So this was the world. Sheesh.

Her father, a bespectacled young man with thinning hair, also dressed in scrubs, kept pointing from the baby to himself as if the crew outside might not be sure this was his daughter. One nurse handed the new father a diaper. He put it on the baby like an expert, then looked through the window where we all applauded him. He grinned sheepishly. A little shirt, a blanket, knit cap, a tiny arm held up for a bye-bye, and the venetian blind closed.

Everyone in the room congratulated the family on their beautiful baby; everyone was sure that their baby would be more beautiful.

"That was really something," Fred said. "I

never got to see ours until they were in the nursery."

"And I was asleep when they were born."

"So was I, thank God." Mary Alice had come up behind us. "This is like squatting in a Laura Ashley field, you ask me."

"Debbie okay?"

"About there, I think. She and Henry don't need me in there."

A very sensitive thing to do, leave the parents alone to share the birth, and I told her so.

"Well, they came in and were cranking up the bed to this ungodly position and I said to myself, 'Mary Alice, it's time to get the hell out of Dodge.' "

"Good thinking," Fred agreed. "Do you think I have time to go to the bathroom?"

"How long does it take you?"

Fred ignored Mary Alice and headed down the hall. She and I sat in two of the straight chairs that were lined up along the middle of the room. Obviously people weren't supposed to stay here long enough to warrant being comfortable.

"Well, what did Virgil have to say?" I asked.

"Monk Crawford died of snakebites."

"You mean it was an accident?"

"Far from it. One whole arm was full of bites. Virgil said he was tied up and it looked like his arm was put down in a basket of snakes. Then they left him to die in the car." She paused. "The snakes were gone, though. Virgil was glad of that."

"Oh, good Lord." I closed my eyes for a

101

moment fighting down nausea. The group that had just welcomed their new baby girl left, wishing us good luck.

"Thanks," Sister said. "And congratulations."

"What about Virginia?" I asked. "You said maybe they had found her."

"They found a sales receipt for the car in the glove compartment. Virginia had sold the car to Holden Crawford."

I thought about this a minute.

"That doesn't mean anything. The Crawford guy could have forced Virginia to write a sales slip so if anyone questioned his having the car he could say he bought it."

"That's true," Sister conceded. "But Virgil said it was a lead."

"Sounds like a lead to another dead body if you ask me."

"Well, I'm thinking maybe she sold the car and went to Disney World."

"She what?" I stared at Sister.

"You know. Like those 'I just won the Super Bowl and I'm going to Disney World' folks. Virginia left Luke, she's feeling good about it, and she's gone to Disney World."

I shook my head in amazement. Somehow my loony sister had segued from a dead snake handler to Mickey Mouse and had lost me in the transition.

"That doesn't make a grain of sense," I said.

"But it's a nice thought. Nicer than the alternative."

I couldn't argue with that.

"Have you heard from Richard?" I asked.

"Not yet." She patted her purse. "Call forwarding."

"Well, you be sure and tell him his mother's at Disney World. I know he'll be relieved."

Fred came back in and Sister told him about Monk Crawford's death. His reaction was the same as mine.

"Snakes? Good Lord! What kind of snakes?"

"Poisonous."

I was glad I was sitting between them, and I was glad that was the moment when a granny-Laura came to the door and said, "Lamont family."

The three of us jumped up and rushed to the window. The venetian blinds were opened just as a beaming Henry came in carrying David Anthony. He kissed him and handed him over to the nurse, who laid him on the table before us.

What can I say? He was quite simply the most beautiful baby I have ever seen in my life. He had a head full of black hair and perfect little features not flattened out like most newborns. Unlike the baby girl who had been on that same table earlier, David Anthony looked around calmly.

We all waved at him.

"You precious."

"You darling."

Fred nudged me. "Look at that, Patricia Anne. He's looking at us." Then, "Hey, you sweet boy."

Henry pointed to the baby and then to himself just like the other father had done earlier.

We nodded. Yes, David Anthony was obviously his. Yes, he was amazing. Yes, he, Henry, had pulled off a miracle.

The eyedrops, diaper, blanket, cap, wave bye-bye. And we were hugging each other and crying. All of the joy, all of the hope in the world was in that small room that January night.

Tears rolled down Sister's cheeks. "He looks just like Will Alec. It's amazing."

It would have been amazing if it were true. Will Alec was husband number one. David Anthony's grandfather was husband number two, Philip Nachman. Oh, well. They were both nice men.

On the way home, after we had spoken to Debbie and told her how wonderful the baby was, I tried to figure out what kin David Anthony would be to Haley's and Philip's baby when (cross your fingers) they had one. Debbie and Haley were first cousins on our side; Debbie and Philip were first cousins on their fathers' side. Third cousins once removed? Double third cousins? Jet lag kicked in and I was sound asleep and drooling when Fred pulled into our driveway.

"Let's call Haley," he said as we walked into the house.

I glanced at the wall clock. "It's five or six o'clock in the morning over there."

"Wake her up with the good news."

But she was awake.

"We already know," she exclaimed. "Aunt Sister's already called. Tell Debbie and Henry that we're toasting the baby with mimosas. More champagne than orange juice. Does he look like the twins?"

"He has a lot of black hair and he's not smushed like some babies."

We talked for a half hour. Thank God for Alexander Graham Bell and satellites. And credit cards.

Chapter Nine

"Mrs. Hollowell?"

"Yes?" I didn't recognize the woman's voice.

"Is this the Mrs. Hollowell who was at Chandler Mountain yesterday?"

I set my coffee cup down so suddenly that coffee sloshed into the saucer and Muffin jumped off the kitchen table. Someone had found Virginia's body.

"Yes." I held my breath.

"Mrs. Hollowell, this is Betsy Mahall. We met yesterday at the Jesus Is Our Life and Heaven Hereafter church."

The girl with the flowers. The murdered girl's sister.

"Betsy, don't tell me something else has happened."

"Oh, no ma'am. Did I scare you? I'm sorry."

"I just thought for a minute that you might be calling about my cousin's wife. She's still missing."

"That's what I heard." There was a pause.

I could hear children arguing in the background. "Just a minute, Mrs. Hollowell. Jamie, give Ethan back his Cookie Monster. Go get one of your own toys." A pause. "Right now, Jamie. I mean it." And then, "I'm sorry, Mrs. Hollowell. They know something is wrong, and all they're doing is squabbling.

"No, nothing else has happened, thank God. What I called about was to see if we could meet somewhere today. There were some things I didn't get to ask you yesterday about my sister. Some important things. And, also, I've got information that might help with your cousin."

"Information about Virginia? You can't tell me on the phone?"

"It's a long story, Mrs. Hollowell. I can't come all the way into Birmingham because of the children. My next-door neighbor can keep them for a while, but not all afternoon. And I hate to ask you to come to Steele. Do you think we could maybe meet in Springville? Maybe for lunch?" She hesitated. "I really wouldn't ask you if it weren't important."

I looked at the wall clock. 9:15.

"Betsy, I just don't know. I may have to go with my sister back up to Oneonta today."

"Mrs. Hollowell, I really need to talk to you." Betsy's voice lowered and she almost whispered, "I'm scared about something."

Scared? What in the world about? And why me? It didn't make sense. I'd only seen the girl one time.

"Please?" A catch in her voice and a barely audible sniff. Betsy was crying.

That got me. The old schoolteacher help-the-kids-out mode kicked in.

"Where in Springville?" I asked. There went all of my plans for the day. The house was a mess. I needed to dust and vacuum. I still hadn't done all of the washing or paid the bills that had stacked up while we were in Warsaw. So much for good intentions.

"You know where that bakery is right on the main street by the library?"

"The one that has some tables outside?"

"That's it. They serve soup and sandwiches. Do you think you could meet me around twelve?"

"I'll be there."

"Thank you, Mrs. Hollowell. Thank you so much."

We said goodbye and I hung up wondering why in the world I had agreed to this. How could I help this girl? All I knew about her was that she was pretty, had long red hair, and was grieving for her snake-handling sister who had been murdered. Also that she was scared.

"What's she scared about?" Sister wanted to know when I called her and told her where I was going. "And what does she think you can do, Mouse?"

"I have no idea. But she said she might have some information about Virginia."

"Well, I hope so. Richard's on his way up to Oneonta now to see about his daddy. He wanted me to go with him and I said I had to take care of Fay and May."

"Richardena, the twin's nanny, is there, isn't she?"

"Oh, sure. But Debbie's coming home this afternoon with David Anthony. Can you believe having a baby one day and coming home the next?"

I could tell that Sister was shaking her head just like I was shaking mine. Each of us had had the luxury of four or five days in the hospital when our children were born.

"Anyway," she continued, "I need to prepare the twins for their little brother."

I decided I didn't want to know about these preparations. No two children had ever been better prepared for the birth of a sibling: Debbie and Henry had seen to that. So I told her I would call her when I got back and let her know what Betsy had to say.

There were still signs of Christmas everywhere, wreaths on doors, a few Santas still poised on roofs. Billboards still wished us HAPPY HOLIDAYS from banks or from the anchors of local TV stations, all smiles and red suits. In some homes, I knew, the trees would stay up, lighted. In February, they would be decorated with Easter eggs, biddies, and bunnies.

Christmas does not depart Birmingham quickly or for long. Maybe on the Fourth of July it takes a vacation long enough to watch the fireworks from Vulcan Park.

I went through downtown Birmingham, through Malfunction Junction where several interstates battle it out and where that day, miraculously, there wasn't a wreck, past the airport exit and onto I-59 North. Traffic wasn't heavy and, though clouds were coming in from the west, the sun was shining and the temperature was in the high fifties. It would rain later, turn cold the next day, and then warm up, the typical January weather pattern. It's seldom that we have more than two nights consecutively when the temperature goes below freezing.

Midmorning, midweek, the interstates are a pleasure to drive, a pleasure that the citizens of Jefferson County and Birmingham didn't have as soon as most large metropolitan areas. Jefferson County didn't vote for George Wallace for governor; the interstates came to the county line and stopped. There's a slight chance that it was a coincidence, but where the interstates suddenly became two-lane roads in congested areas, we had what became known as the George Corley Wallace Memorial Bottlenecks. Fred and I would take the kids to visit his parents in Montgomery, an hour-and-a-half drive, and sit at the bottleneck on Highway 31 for an hour trying to get back into Birmingham. Not conducive to family harmony.

That morning there was no bottleneck, though. Nothing but the rolling Appalachians and the deep cuts through the limestone that forms them. Some of the views were breathtaking, and I realized how seldom I noticed them. But, of course, I was usually with Mary Alice.

The Springville exit overlooks a large farmpond. A sign at the top of the exit pointed right and declared, FISHING, $2 A DAY. So far no one had paid the two dollars; the pond, shimmering in the January sunlight, was deserted. Several cows were in the pasture, though, some of them grazing, some lying down, a sure sign of rain within a few hours.

The entrance to Springville is much like the entrance into Steele, the same railroad track, the main street of business, the old houses. Springville is much closer to Birmingham, though, and has become one of its principal bedroom communities. Just beyond the main street, developments with names like McDonald's Farms have sprung up for the young professionals who want the small-town life and don't mind the commute to Birmingham.

I glanced at my watch. I was a few minutes early and thought I would sit at one of the tables in the sun and wait for Betsy. But as I parked, I saw her get out of her car and go into the bakery. Her bright red hair was pulled back into a single plait that reached almost to her waist, and for a second I saw that same hair tumbling over a church pew. Damn.

The bakery was attractive, decorated in blue and white with starched lace curtains and a blue ceramic Dutch shoe holding three almost real-looking white tulips on each of the six tables. Only three of the tables had people sitting at them. Takeout seemed to be the bakery's big business. There was a line at the cash register, each person holding a sack that proclaimed OLDE HOLLAND BAKERY. The smells were wonderful.

Betsy was already sitting in a chair just inside the doorway, one of two chairs placed there for the obvious purpose of waiting. She looked up and smiled when she saw me.

"Thank you," she said, as if she were relieved that I had shown up.

"You're welcome." That wasn't the right answer, but it sufficed.

Betsy stood up, no taller than my own five feet, I noticed. But she was more beautiful than I had realized the day before. In spite of her eyes being slightly puffy, their clear hazel was startling. She had the very fair skin that some redheads are blessed with, and a few freckles across her nose.

"We have to order at the counter," she said, pointing to a chalkboard on the wall with the day's menu on it. "They've got lentil soup today. They make the best in the world."

"Sounds good."

We each ordered a bowl of soup and decided we would split a club sandwich. While we were waiting for our food, we sat at a table by the window. The sun was still shining across the table, but a glance at the sky showed the progression of the dark wall of clouds.

Neither of us spoke for a moment. It was noisy in the bakery and I was about to suggest that we go sit at one of the tables outside. As long as the sun was shining, we would be comfortable.

But before I could make the suggestion, Betsy leaned forward and said, "I want to tell you about my sister."

I nodded. This wasn't what I had expected, but talking about her sister was probably something she needed to do.

"Susan was fifteen and I was eighteen when our parents were killed in a small plane. They had gone to Florida for the weekend with another couple, the couple who owned the plane. They ran into a thunderstorm." Betsy picked up the salt shaker (a pink pig with holes in its head) and examined it as if there were some meaning there. She sighed, set it down, and continued.

"I was a freshman at the university, and Susan went to live with our aunt Pearl, our father's sister. She was a widow and had never had any children, and she and Susan grew very close."

I began to get the picture.

"Your aunt Pearl. She was a snake handler?"

Betsy nodded. "The sweetest, kindest person who ever lived. She and my father were raised in a strict Baptist family just like Susan and I were. But Aunt Pearl wanted more. She wasn't satisfied with what she called 'diluted religion.' At least that's what Susan said. She told me once that Aunt Pearl said she wanted to touch God."

By handling snakes? But I nodded.

Betsy picked up the salt shaker again. "I didn't know anything about it, what Aunt Pearl was doing. I imagine our parents did, but they never said anything to us. Even after they were killed and I came home for Christmas or spring break, Susan and Aunt Pearl kept what was going on a secret from me."

She looked up. "I don't know why Aunt Pearl never tried to proselytize me. But she didn't. Just Susan."

"You were older. Your beliefs were already established."

"I guess so." Betsy managed a smile. "Or maybe it was simply that she knew how scared I was of snakes."

The smile faded. "But, you know, that's part of it. You're scared to death, but you handle them anyway, thinking your faith will protect you."

"Which Susan believed."

Betsy nodded. "Which Susan believed. And Aunt Pearl, too. She died just three years after our parents did. Throat cancer. But by that time, Susan had married Ethan. She married him when she was seventeen. She met him at the church, of course. He was Monk Crawford's son."

Tears suddenly rolled down Betsy's face. She reached for a paper napkin and held it against her face.

"I'm sorry, Mrs. Hollowell. It just hits me every now and then that Susan's gone."

"You stayed close?"

She nodded, the napkin still pressed to her eyes.

"In spite of everything. We just didn't talk about that part of her life." Betsy crumpled the napkin in her hand and looked out of the window. "Except once. When Ethan was killed, she asked me to take care of the children if anything happened to her. Which meant that she wasn't going to give up the handling. And, Lord knows, after what happened to Ethan, it was obvious to her how dangerous it was."

It hadn't been a dangerous rattlesnake that had killed Susan, but I didn't say anything.

"And of course I said yes. I love those children better than anything in the world. Terry does, too."

"Do you have children of your own?"

"We do now." A weak smile and a swipe of the napkin under her eyes. "I'm sorry. I know I'm embarrassing you. Do you want to go sit at the tables outside?"

"You're not embarrassing me. Don't worry about that."

Betsy sighed. "I know you can't understand, I don't understand myself, but Susan was such a sensible person in so many ways. Such a loving person."

No, I didn't, couldn't understand such need, such religious fervor. What would it be like to want to touch God? To hold up a snake? I shivered.

They called our number and Betsy said, "I'll get it."

I watched her get the tray and collect napkins and plastic spoons from a side counter. She looked like a child, I realized, with the long plait almost to the waist of her jeans. She had draped her denim jacket across the back of her chair, and her simple yellow shirt emphasized how small she was.

"Here we go." Betsy placed the bowl of soup in front of me and handed me a spoon and napkin. "I think you'll like this. It's so hot, you might want to put some ice in it."

We both scooped some ice from our tea with the plastic spoons and dropped it into our soup. It melted immediately.

"Do you work, Betsy?" I asked.

She nodded. "At the telephone company. I called yesterday and I think I can take maternity leave. They allow for special circumstances."

She passed a basket of crackers to me.

"They're going to be surprised when they get a request from me for maternity leave."

I took a package of crackers and looked at her questioningly.

"Terry and I have been married eight years. We've tried it all, even in vitro a couple of times. We've given up."

"Will you adopt Susan's children?"

"Of course. It's what she would have wanted."

I was doing some mental calculations while I was opening the crackers.

"Susan married before you did, didn't she? She waited a while to have children."

Betsy nodded. "Midtwenties. That's what I meant about her being sensible in so many ways."

She took her first sip of the soup. "Umm, good. But still hot. Be careful, Mrs. Hollowell."

She was right. The lentil soup was delicious. For a few minutes we concentrated on eating. At least I was eating. Betsy was stirring her soup, lifting an occasional spoonful.

The sun disappeared suddenly from our table. The wall of clouds had made it halfway across the sky.

"Susan's funeral is in the morning at eleven," Betsy said listlessly as if the sudden shadow had reminded her. "We're having it at the funeral home, not at the church."

"What about Holden Crawford's?" I asked.

"They haven't released the body yet." She shivered. "You know how he died, don't you?"

"I heard."

Another stir of the soup.

"Well, what I wanted to tell you about your cousin was that Monk never would have hurt her. Chances are that she's okay somewhere."

"But he was found dead in her car."

"That's what I heard."

Betsy put her spoon down and touched a napkin to her mouth. "I want to tell you about Monk."

"Okay."

"He wasn't educated, grew up poor as dirt on a tenant farm up near Scottsboro, but he was a good man. A man who believed in his church and his family."

I nodded and Betsy continued.

"He built that church up there on Chandler Mountain and was known all over the Southeast as one of the leading preachers and handlers."

Known all over the Southeast? How had I missed out on all of this?

"But when his wife died and then Ethan, he lost his faith," Susan said. "Got bitten by a timber rattler last summer at a brush-arbor meeting in Tennessee. Almost died."

I interrupted her. "What's a brush-arbor?"

"It's like a makeshift church. The handlers don't have too many real churches or places to meet so in the summertime they build brush-arbors, they call them. Vines and branches. Maybe put plastic over the top. Maybe not. Just temporary places to have meetings.

"Anyway, Monk nearly died, said God had turned his back on him."

Betsy lifted a spoonful of soup to her mouth and tasted it thoughtfully.

"Like I said, Susan and I didn't talk about it much, but she told me that Monk had quit handling and was gone most of the time, house painting. She was worried about the church."

"The church?"

"Apparently there's a lot of politics involved just like in everything. Several people were eager to take Monk's place."

"As head snake handler." I sounded more cynical than I had intended.

But Betsy didn't take offense.

"Including Susan, I'm sure," she said.

She gave up trying to eat and pushed her food away. "I know it sounds crazy, but I'm sure she was that involved. And I'm sure that's why she and Monk both were killed. Susan was a woman and Monk had lost his faith. The handlers don't take kindly to either."

"Women aren't supposed to handle?"

"They can. They're kept in subservient roles, though. Have to dress in long dresses, answer when their husbands crook their fingers. That kind of thing."

I thought of the outfit Susan had worn in the church. The long skirt, how neatly it had been arranged around her. Was it possible that she had been killed in this day and age for being an "uppity" woman?

"Oh, I almost forgot."

Betsy reached in her purse, which was hanging on the knob of the chair.

"I found this at Susan's house yesterday. I think it may belong to your cousin. Her name is Virginia, isn't it?"

"Virginia Nelson."

I took the piece of paper that Betsy held out to me. On it was written "Virginia N. (206) 555-0105."

"It was by the phone in Susan's kitchen."

206? I wondered where that area code was. And if this was really a lead to Luke's Virginia. Virginia, even Virginia N. was a common name.

"Thanks," I said, slipping the paper in my purse.

"I hope you find her there. Like I said, she's somewhere and all right, though. Monk wouldn't have hurt her."

But someone had definitely hurt Monk and his daughter-in-law. Perhaps Virginia had been at the wrong place at the wrong time?

"And what I wanted to ask you about Susan was if you saw a cameo on her? She always wore a cameo on a long gold chain. Always. It belonged to our grandmother. I got her ring and Susan got her cameo. Susan said it was her talisman."

"I didn't see anything like that. She was lying on her stomach, though. It could have been under her."

"Well, nobody brought it to me when they brought me her purse. And I looked all over her house for it."

Tears welled again.

"She wouldn't have been without it, Mrs. Hollowell. And it belongs to Jamie now."

What could I say? "I didn't see it, Betsy. I'm sorry."

"I am, too. I was just hoping that you might remember. It's an unusual, beautiful cameo. If you'd seen it, then I'd know that it disappeared somewhere between the church and the morgue and I could start tracing. I'm so worried that it's gone."

"You said when you called that you were scared."

She dipped the plastic spoon into the soup again and stirred.

"I'm just scared the cameo is lost, that someone has taken it."

An old schoolteacher knows a liar when she sees one. And Betsy was lying. The plastic spoon shook; she let go of it.

"You're sure?" I was leaving the door open if she wanted to tell me what was really worrying her.

"Yes."

I reached across the table and took her hand, which was clenched into a fist.

"The cameo will show up."

"I'll keep my fingers crossed."

Be careful what you wish for.

Chapter Ten

Area code 206. The first thing I did when I got home was look in the telephone directory. Seattle? Virginia had gone to Seattle? Surely not. It must be the telephone number for a different Virginia. Not that Seattle wouldn't be a lovely city to visit, but it was a long way from Columbus, Mississippi.

Did she have relatives out there that I hadn't heard of? Friends?

Well, there was one way to find out.

I picked up the phone and dialed the number. It was answered by a recorded male voice informing me that I had reached the Gordon residence, that they were unable to answer the phone, and that if I would leave my name and number, they would return my call.

I hung up. Obviously a wrong number. I thumbtacked it to the kitchen bulletin board, though. Luke and Richard could pursue it if they wanted to.

Which reminded me. I dialed Sister's number to see if she had heard from either of them.

Tiffany answered. Ms. Crane had gone shopping. At the Big, Bold, and Beautiful Shoppe, she thought, and no, ma'am, Mr. Nelson hadn't called. A Sheriff Stuckey had, though, two times.

"Did he sound like it was an emergency?"

"Oh, no, ma'am. I think he just wanted to know if she got the flowers he sent her. I told him they were here but she hadn't seen them yet. I told him they're beautiful and I knew she would appreciate them."

"What kind are they?"

"All different kinds. Lilies and tulips and daisies and stuff. Mostly purple. They're beautiful."

"Sounds like it."

"The card says, 'My heart leapt up, Virgil.' Isn't that sweet?"

"Leapt?"

"Like leaped, Mrs. Hollowell. That's the way poets say leaped. Leapt."

"Oh, okay. Well, tell Mary Alice to call me when she gets in. And have you heard from Debbie and the baby this afternoon?"

"Henry called and said they aren't coming home until tomorrow. The baby has a little jaundice and they're putting him under lights. Everything's going to be fine, though." She paused. "I heard the stress ball worked great."

"Like a charm."

I told her goodbye, hung up, and called Debbie. Everything really was okay. Brother just had a touch of jaundice. Nothing to worry about.

"Brother?"

Debbie giggled. "Well, Henry brought the twins over this morning, and that's what they called him. Isn't it cute?"

It was. A good Southern name. Brother Lamont. So much for David Anthony. The child would be Brother for the rest of his life.

I turned on the Weather Channel. It looked like it might rain at any minute, but the radar showed that the rain had just crossed the Mississippi-Alabama border. I threw on some sweats and a jacket and got Woofer's leash. If I didn't take him for a walk then, we wouldn't get one in that day.

He was curled up in his igloo, but he came out eagerly when I rattled the leash. Back in the fall, he had been bitten by a possum and had been very sick. Something good had come of it, though. When I took him back for his checkup, the vet had noticed how stiff he was and had prescribed some new arthritis medicine they've developed for dogs. Woofer can hike his leg halfway up a telephone pole now to mark his territory.

"Good old boy," I said, putting the leash on. "Good old Woofer."

I didn't even have to coax him to the gate.

A few drops of rain had begun to fall as we returned, and the temperature had dropped ten or fifteen degrees. There had been no mention of wintry precipitation in the weather forecast, but the drops felt icy. It was hard to realize that just a few hours earlier Betsy and I could have sat in the sun at the Olde Holland Bakery and not been uncomfortable.

I took Woofer's leash off, gave him a couple of dog biscuits, and hurried toward the house. Just as I reached the back porch, Mary Alice opened the gate.

"Hey," she called. "Wait 'til you see what I bought." She held up several Big, Bold, and Beautiful plastic garment bags.

I held the kitchen door open for her.

"Whew," she said, going into the den and draping the bags over a chair. "I'm worn out. I've been shopping all day."

"I thought you were going to prepare the twins for their new brother."

"Well, I was. But he's not coming home until tomorrow so there's no hurry. They're putting him under those bake lights."

"So I heard."

"They had to do the same thing for Debbie. Remember? It must be a Nachman gene."

"Must be. You want a Coke?"

"Lord, yes." She was taking the plastic from a purple pants suit as I went into the kitchen.

"Have you talked to Tiffany?" I called over the crunch of the ice falling into the glasses. "Did you know you have some flowers?"

"Really?" She came into the kitchen holding the purple suit over her arm. "Who from?"

"Guess. He said his heart leapt up."

Joy leapt into her face. "Virgil?"

"Yep. His heart leapt." I put the Cokes on the kitchen table and reached in the cabinet for a package of oatmeal cookies, which I also placed on the table.

"Tiffany says he's called a couple of times, too."

"I declare."

Suddenly she frowned.

"He didn't say anything was wrong, did he?"

"Tiffany said he just wanted to know if you got the flowers."

"Well, bless his heart." She held up the suit. "You like this?"

"It's beautiful. No telling what Virgil's heart will do."

Sister giggled, laid the suit over a kitchen chair, and sat down at the table.

"Have you heard from Richard or Luke?" I asked her.

"Not yet. I told Richard that if they let Luke out, they could come to my house."

"Well, I may have a lead on where Virginia is."

Sister stuck a whole cookie in her mouth. "Ditny Wull?"

I took the card from the bulletin board and handed it to her.

"This is a Seattle number. I called it and got a machine saying the Gordon residence."

Sister studied the card while she chewed, swallowed, and took a drink of Coke. "Where did you get this?"

"Betsy Mahall. The girl we saw yesterday at the church on Chandler Mountain? The dead girl's sister? I told you I was having lunch with her today."

"I'd forgotten. What did she have to say?"

"She told me how her sister got started snake handling and that she was sure Virginia was all right, that Monk Crawford was a kind man."

"Well, a dead one, anyway. Where did she get this card?"

"She said it was by her sister's phone, and she thought it might be our Virginia."

I took a cookie from the package.

"She wanted to know if we noticed whether or not her sister was wearing a cameo, a big one on a long gold chain. I said I didn't see one. Did you?"

"You mean in the church? I didn't look. Why?"

"It's missing and she says her sister always wore it, that it was her grandmother's and she wants her sister's little girl to have it." I bit into the cookie. "She's going to raise the two children."

"Don't talk with your mouth full, Mouse."

I stuck out my tongue.

"Lord, don't do that. Mama's turning over in her grave."

I closed my mouth and swallowed before I said, "Betsy thinks someone at the church killed the Crawford guy and her sister. She says Monk Crawford had been the undisputed leader of that whole bunch for years, but had lost his faith and wouldn't handle serpents anymore. And women take a secondary role so they wouldn't have wanted her sister to take his place."

"I'm sure Virgil will solve it," she said smugly. Oh, the faith of the smitten.

"Well, I hope he talks to Betsy. I think she knows more than she told me. On the phone she said she was scared, but at the restaurant she acted like she was just worried because the cameo was gone."

"What would she be scared of? She's not one of the handlers."

"I don't know," I admitted. "Maybe it has something to do with the children." I sipped my Coke and thought about the possibilities. "If Monk Crawford owned that house then maybe he owned the church, too. Or the land it's on, anyway. And the children will inherit it. And someone might not want them to."

"That doesn't make sense," Sister said.

I had to admit that she was right.

After I had admired Sister's clothes and heard the latest about our friend Bonnie Blue Butler, manager of the Big, Bold, and Beautiful Shoppe (she had met a man over Christmas, a downright hunk), I copied down the phone number that Betsy had given me that might be Virginia's, told her goodbye, took a carton of Brunswick stew from the freezer for supper, and collapsed on the sofa under an afghan. The next thing I knew, Fred woke me up by turning a lamp on.

"What time is it?" I asked, confused.

"A little after six and it's sleeting. There are already wrecks everywhere. That's why I'm late. There's a six-car pileup down at Wildwood Shopping Center."

He put a cold hand against my arm. I flinched.

"Told you it was cold."

"I believe you."

"You want to warm me up?"

I raised the afghan; he pulled off his shoes and slid in beside me.

"Lord, you *are* cold."

"Um."

We lay there listening to the click of sleet on the skylights, to the hum of the furnace.

"Good day?" I murmured.

"Um."

When we woke up, it was nine o'clock and

126

the phone was ringing. Fred reached backward and picked it up from the end table.

"What?" More of a bark than a question.

He handed me the phone and sat up. "It's your sister."

"Hey," I said, watching Fred get up and shuffle toward the kitchen.

"What's going on?" Mary Alice asked. "Y'all having a fight?"

"No. We were asleep on the sofa. Jet lag may have taken a permanent toll."

"Well, turn on Channel 6. Virgil's going to be on it in a few minutes talking about the murders. He says he's going to be on CNN, too, but he doesn't know when. When I find out, I'm going to call Haley and tell her to watch him."

I was still groggy. "CNN?"

"I guess because it's so exotic killing someone with snakes."

"Well, don't tell her we found the body in the church. I didn't. I don't want to worry her."

"I'll just tell her to watch for Virgil."

"Haley will be thrilled that Alabama made the international news again."

Sister missed the sarcasm totally.

"I'm sure she will. Y'all turn on Channel 6 now."

Fred came back through the den and headed for the bathroom.

"Are Richard and Luke at your house?" I asked Sister.

"Richard is. They're going to keep Luke another day or two in the hospital. Richard is such a nice young man, Mouse. Oh, and incidentally, he called that number in Seattle and talked to the people. They don't know who in the world Virginia is. Mrs. Gordon said she's got a daughter who lives in Biloxi, though. Small world, isn't it?"

"Thanks to CNN."

"Turn on Channel 6. The news is coming on right now."

I reached for the remote.

The first story was the weatherman apologizing for missing the forecast. Cold air had moved in earlier than expected overriding warm Gulf air. Some wintry precipitation. No accumulation. No big deal. I glanced up at the skylights. They were frozen solid. I would have to get the candles out.

The next story was the murders. Side-by-side pictures of Monk and Susan Crawford were flashed on the screen. A shot of Virginia's car on a dirt road near Pulaski came on while the reporter explained that Holden Crawford, a snake-handling preacher from Chandler Mountain, had died from multiple snakebites just one day after the body of his daughter-in-law Susan had been found in the church where they practiced their religious rituals. Foul play was suspected.

No kidding.

"Come here, Fred," I yelled. "I want you to see this."

"I'm here," he said. I hadn't heard him come back in.

"They're fixing to show Virgil Stuckey, the guy who has a crush on Sister."

And they did. Sheriff Virgil Stuckey of St.

128

Clair County was introduced. He was standing by the car, too, and the reporter asked if it was true that Holden Crawford had been bitten over a hundred times by snakes. Then she stuck her mike in his face.

"I'm sorry," he said. "We can't release any of the details yet."

"But Holden Crawford was a well-known snake handler, wasn't he?"

"Yes, he was."

"And his daughter-in-law was, too?"

"Yes."

"Thank you, Sheriff Stuckey."

The report then segued to Chandler Mountain and an ancient woman introduced as Aunt Beulah Packard who said it was the Chandler Mountain booger got them both, that Lord Jesus, you ought to hear that thing howling at night. Howling for blood, you asked her.

She picked up a tin can by her chair and the camera moved a second before the Channel 6 audience was treated to her spitting snuff into the can.

"What on God's earth?" Fred asked.

I couldn't remember how much I had told him. Apparently not much. He sat at the kitchen table saying, "What? What?" while I told him the whole story and scrambled us some eggs. The Brunswick stew I put back in the freezer. I know you're not supposed to refreeze food, but if I nuked it long enough, it should kill the bacteria. And it was too late for spicy food.

"Don't you get messed up in this, Patricia Anne. These sound like strange people."

I handed him some buttered toast. "Betsy Mahall, Susan Crawford's sister, isn't strange. She and her husband, Terry, are going to raise Susan's children."

"Well, it's good the children have somebody."

I nodded. "Somebody who really wants them."

The lights went out just as we were finishing our eggs. And I hadn't checked since I got home to see if we had an E-mail from Haley. Given our track record with electricity, it could be days before I could use the computer.

"She'll be home in two months," Fred said, reading my thoughts.

This time we lucked out. The lights were back on the next morning, had been off only four hours. Ice still coated our skylight and deck, though, and a fine mist was falling, almost like a fog, coating the tops of pine trees. I slid across the deck with Woofer's breakfast, a good way to break a hip, but I had to see if he was all right.

Which, of course, he was. Snug and happy in his igloo, money well spent.

I was watching Virgil Stuckey on TV, a repeat of the story of the night before, when Fred came into the den, dressed for work.

"The roads are too icy for you to go out," I exclaimed when I saw him. "Wait a while. It's supposed to get above freezing during the morning."

"I called Mark. He's got a four-wheel drive. He's going to pick me up."

Mark Taylor was a young man who worked

for Fred. A very nice young man whose hobby happened to be stock-car racing, a fact which didn't comfort me on an icy morning.

"It'll be fine." He pointed to the TV and Virgil Stuckey. "That guy looks just like Willard Scott."

A few minutes later, I watched nervously as he slid across the deck. The sound of Mark's car motor roaring in our driveway was not comforting.

"You call me when you get there and don't you let Mark drive fast."

"Don't worry."

Yeah. I closed the door, picked Muffin up, and went into the boys' old bedroom where I had set up the computer.

"Maybe we've got a message from your Mama," I told the cat.

We did.

E-MAIL
FROM: HALEY
TO: MAMA AND PAPA
SUBJECT: DAVID ANTHONY

David Anthony is so precious. I wish I were there. The picture is great, but I want to hold him. He doesn't look much like Fay and May, does he? All that dark hair. All they had was a little fuzz. And of course he's a lot larger than they were, those beautiful tiny girls. Philip says he looks like Uncle Philip, his grandaddy. We've been trying to figure out if we have children what kin they will be to

David Anthony since both of us are Debbie's first cousins. Confusing, isn't it? And nice.
 I love you,
  Haley

PS. Tell Aunt Sister I just saw Virgil Stuckey on CNN. He reminds me of somebody I know, but I can't put my finger on exactly who. Snake handlers? Lord!
PPS. How's Luke?

E-MAIL
FROM: MAMA
TO: HALEY
SUBJECT: BROTHER LAMONT

Darling,
 David Anthony is now Brother. We should have known.
 Love,
  Mama
 It's icy here today. Not like Warsaw, but Birmingham icy. The worst kind.

I hit the send button, rubbed Muffin between her ears, and looked out at the mist, ice motes suspended in the air. In a couple of hours, Betsy Mahall would be burying her sister Susan. On such a morning.

I clicked on the WHITE PAGES and typed in TERRY MAHALL in STEELE, ALABAMA. The message came back that there was no such person listed. I typed in TERRENCE and the number and address came up. So easy. And to think I had lived for sixty years without a computer.

132

"Betsy?" I said when she answered. "This is Patricia Anne Hollowell. I just wanted you to know that I'm thinking about you this morning."

"Mrs. Hollowell. Oh, Mrs. Hollowell, thank you so much." A pause and then a long breath. "Everything's icy up here. Terry thinks we ought to put it off. It's a graveside service. But I don't want to. It's like I'm caught somewhere and so is Susan."

"Then do what you need to do."

"I need to put her to rest."

"I know you do. And you're in my thoughts."

"Thank you, Mrs. Hollowell. Thank you for calling. I appreciate it more than you know."

I hung up and looked out of the window until Fred called saying he was safe.

Chapter Eleven

At the age of thirty-nine, Richard Nelson, Luke and Virginia's only child, is a handsome man. Especially, Mary Alice says, since they tacked his ears to his head. Every time she says it, I get a painful vision of a hammer and upholstery tacks. The truth was that Richard's ears did stick out so far when he was a child, that light would shine through them, and our kids were under threats of painful punishment if they called him "Dumbo," which I'm sure they sneaked around and did.

The Richard who sat in my kitchen later that day had grown to match his rather large nose, though, had neat ears attached to his head, and was a very handsome man. He looked more like an L.L. Bean cowboy wanna-be than a congressman in his denim shirt, jeans, and boots. Which was fine. He looked good. I'm sure he had carried most of the female votes in Columbus. I hate to admit it, but it's so much easier to vote for a good-looking man, even one with bird brains. The people of his district were lucky that Richard was smart.

"The problem is Mama's car, Cousin Pat," he was saying. "Sheriff Stuckey said they're going to release it tomorrow in Pulaski and I need to go get it. Cousin Sister said she would take me up there so I could drive it back to Birmingham, but Daddy's getting out of the hospital tomorrow, hopefully."

"I'll go get your daddy, Richard," I volunteered. "Don't give that another thought."

I placed a cup of coffee in front of him and handed him the sugar bowl. "You want a cookie?"

"No, ma'am." He put a couple of teaspoons of sugar in his coffee and stirred it.

I poured myself a cup and sat down across from him. I had finally had time that morning to clean the house, and the comforting noise of tumbling clothes came from the utility room.

"How come you're going to get the car?" I asked. "I thought it belonged to Holden Craw-

134

ford, the guy who was killed, that there was a bill of sale in the glove compartment."

"There was. A handwritten bill of sale. The sale hadn't been recorded."

Richard picked up his coffee and took a sip. "Um. Hot."

The steam should have alerted him to that fact.

"And the handwritten bill won't suffice?"

"Ordinarily it would. But Mr. Holden is dead and Mama's disappeared, so we don't know the circumstances of the sale. We need Mama to say she wrote it, that she actually received the money from Mr. Crawford."

He took another sip of coffee, whispered, "Whew, that's hot," and said, "Mama. Therein lies the problem."

Therein lay part of the problem; there were a couple of bodies lying around, too, which were problematic.

"And you don't have any idea where your mother might have gone?"

"Beats me." He shrugged and put his coffee down. "I thought she and Daddy were getting along fine. Christmas she seemed happier than I'd seen her in a long time."

But Holden Crawford hadn't come to paint their house until after Christmas. Hmmm.

"Happy how?"

"You know. Smiley. Not bugging me all the time to get married."

Richard had had an unfortunate marriage right out of high school to a girl who was employed at the Boobie Bungalow. Enough said. Fortunately, the people of Columbus had forgiven him. And Richard had worked hard to remain a bachelor.

Now he said, "I should have known something was wrong."

"Don't blame yourself." I poured Coffee-mate into my cup and watched it swirl out. "What about that phone number I gave Sister? The Gordons in Seattle."

He shook his head. "They didn't know what I was talking about. Daddy hadn't heard of them, either. He still swears he saw Mama up at that snake-handling church where you found the dead girl."

I looked at the clock. Susan's funeral should be over by now. The freezing drizzle had stopped here in Birmingham. I hoped it had up in Steele.

"You didn't have any trouble coming off the mountain from Sister's, did you?"

"You mean the ice? No, it's melting. I'm used to driving on icy streets in D.C., anyway."

Ice was ice, Birmingham or Washington. Slippery as hell. But I didn't say anything.

"About the car, though," Richard continued. "I sure don't want it. I'd be expecting a snake to crawl out from under the seat all the time. But it's a nice car. Leather seats. Not too many miles."

"But what if it was a legitimate sale?"

"Then the Crawford family can have it. I don't know why they would want it, though. Seems like every time they got in it they'd think of that guy being eaten alive by snakes." He shivered as if a rabbit had run over his grave. "God, I can't think of anything worse. Talk about your nightmares."

"They could sell it. There are two small children involved who are going to have to be raised and educated. I'm sure anything would help."

"I suppose so."

"Are you going up to Oneota to see your daddy today?"

Richard nodded. "In a little while." He sipped his coffee. "You know what I'd like to do? I'd like to take a look at that church and house, see if any of Mama's stuff is there."

He looked at me. "Do you think there's any chance that Daddy really saw Mama?"

"I don't know how."

I explained how the church was sitting against a huge rock and how we could have seen anyone who came out through the side or front door.

"Couldn't you have looked away for a minute or just not have been paying attention?"

"I suppose."

I knew he desperately wanted to find his mother, to know that she was safe.

"I'll tell you what," I said, as much to appease him as anything else. "I'll call the lady who probably has the key to the house. They're having her sister's funeral today and I don't think we could get up the mountain anyway in the ice. But we can go day after tomorrow and you can look around. Maybe we'll find something that'll tell us where your mama is."

I didn't believe it for a minute, but it seemed to make Richard feel better.

"Maybe Daddy will feel like going with us," he said.

A concussed, seeing-double Pukey Lukey going around those mountain curves in Mary Alice's Jag? Or my Chevy?

"What kind of rental car do you have?" I asked.

After Richard left, and after I had folded the clothes, grateful to have everything clean, I decided to go to the library. Cars were passing by the house every few minutes. The roads should be no problem.

What I was looking for was a book by Dennis Covington, a Birmingham native. Entitled *Salvation on Sand Mountain*, it was about snake handling and had been one of the top three finalists for the National Book Award several years earlier. Everyone had said how wonderful it was, but the subject hadn't appealed to me. Now it did. I wanted to know how people like Holden Crawford, his son Ethan, and his daughter-in-law Susan could be drawn into what seemed to me such a bizarre religious practice.

The book was checked out.

"You haven't read that book yet?" Edna Thomas, the librarian asked me. "You don't know what you've missed. You need to go buy it, Patricia Anne."

Which I did. I stopped by Alabama Book-smith and got the same reaction.

"You haven't read that book yet? You don't know what you've missed."

Several hours later, I did. I had missed an

incredible insight into a world I had known nothing about. I had also learned how one could be drawn into this strange world where one celebrated and tested his faith by handling snakes and drinking strychnine. I was so mesmerized that the phone had rung a couple of times and I had let it ring. The answering machine would pick it up.

Handling the snakes and not being bitten proved that you were powerful. That you were in God's favor.

Scary.

When I finally put the book down, I knew one thing. What I had thought impossible, that Virginia Nelson from the Lutheran Church and the country club could be drawn into such a group, wasn't impossible. Like Betsy's Aunt Pearl, she could have been carried away in religious fervor, believed this was the way to touch God, the way to redemption.

Night had fallen, and it was very cold. I walked into the kitchen and turned the back light on. The outside thermometer was sitting on thirty-two.

I threw on a jacket, went out and got Woofer, and brought him into the house for company. When Fred came in, I hugged him so tightly and for so long, I surprised him. I felt as if I had been away from home and from him for a long, long time. And several times during the night, I woke up, listened to his breathing, and watched the shadows on the wall cast by the streetlight.

Needless to say, I woke up with a headache. I downed a couple of aspirin and looked out at a world of light. Ice still coated everything, and a bright sun was bouncing off every crystal of that ice. Bouncing, ping, right between my eyes.

I groaned, crawled back into bed, and pulled the quilt over my head.

"You all right?" Fred asked. I could hear the whir of his electric shaver and knew he was doing his morning routine of wandering around the house while he shaved.

"Headache."

"You want some aspirin?"

"Just took some." I drifted back into a deep sleep.

Two hours later I woke up again, this time feeling much better. A look through the window rewarded me with bright sunshine, melting ice, and no pain.

Muffin was stretched out on the kitchen table in the sun. She answered with a yawn when I told her good morning.

"Lazy cat," I said.

She narrowed her eyes. Who was I to call her lazy? Hadn't I just crawled out of bed?

I glanced at the clock. Almost ten. I poured a cup of the coffee that Fred had made, went into the den, and called Luke at the Blount County Medical Center.

He had been dressed and waiting for me for an hour. Where was I?

"I'll be there at one o'clock," I said. Damned if I was going to hurry.

"But I told them I'd be gone before lunch."

"One o'clock," I repeated. "Are you still seeing double?"

"Just sometimes. Most of the time not. I've got to get out of here, though. I ran into a man who knows Virginia, who saw her up there at that church."

"What do you mean he saw her up there? Is he one of the snake handlers?"

"I don't know. He just came in and said he saw my wife."

"How did he know you were looking for her?"

"Hell, Patricia Anne. I didn't ask him that. He said she was all right, though. Said his name was Thomas Benson. Old man. Here for dialysis."

Probably blew his kidneys on strychnine and snake venom.

"Did you ask him if he knew where she is now?"

"He said he didn't. He said some other folks up there might know, though. He said a lot of them were going to a big meeting up in West Virginia this weekend, so we need to get up there real quick, Patricia Anne, and ask around."

"Did he give you any names, Luke? We can't just go up to a door and knock and ask if they saw Virginia or if they're snake handlers. It's against the law you know."

"Asking about your wife?"

"Snake-handling, Luke." He wasn't being too quick here.

"Then how come they don't arrest them?"

"I think they have to be endangering others."

"Well, hell, Patricia Anne. That's what they're doing carrying those copper-tailed-rattle-mouthed-moccasins around."

"One o'clock, Luke." I hung up and went to take a shower.

I hadn't checked my messages the night before, so as soon as I dried my hair, I turned them on. An invitation to join the Angel Sighting Society, a reminder of a dental appointment (damn, I'd forgotten that), and Mitzi from next door. She had a present for David Anthony and she and Arthur wanted to see our Warsaw pictures.

Hell, I hadn't even had them developed.

I called her, apologized for not getting back sooner, halfway explained what had been going on, told her that David Anthony was now Brother, and invited her to go to Oneonta with me to get Luke.

"Pukey Lukey? You're driving him home from the hospital?"

"Yep."

I thought I heard a snicker.

"Patricia Anne, much as I'd love to keep you company, I can't do it today. I've got all sorts of running around to do."

I didn't blame her.

At one o'clock, straight up, I walked into Luke's room. He looked at his watch.

"They brought me lunch."

"Good." At least I hoped it was. "You're ready then?" I asked.

"All I've got is this Georgia suitcase." He

held up a plastic Rich's bag. "Richard brought me some pajamas and clean clothes."

Guilt. I should have remembered that he needed things like toiletries and pajamas and that his clothes had been covered in blood.

"You're checked out?"

"Had to promise them my first-born child. Damn, Patricia Anne. You been in a hospital lately?"

"No, thank God. Do they have to take you out in a wheelchair?"

"I suppose." Luke mashed the call button.

"Yes?" came a disembodied female voice.

"My cousin's here to get me."

"Okay. Be right there."

I looked at Luke. He was pale but not exceptionally so. The only strange thing about his appearance was a red streak across the top of each cheekbone as if someone had applied blush and not brushed it out evenly.

He noticed me looking.

"You see these?" He ran his fingers across each cheek. "Allergic reaction to the dye they put in me to do a brain scan. Had to give me shots of antihistamines."

"Is it going to be okay?" I didn't want to be halfway to Birmingham and have him go into anaphylactic shock.

"Oh, sure. It's about gone. Yesterday I was red from the neck up, though. That Thomas Benson fellow said I looked like I'd been snakebit."

"So he was a snake handler."

"I guess so. I didn't get into it with him."

"Do you think he might be here today? Maybe we could talk to him some more."

Luke shook his head. "He comes in three times a week, he said. He'll probably be back tomorrow or the next day."

An orderly came in with a wheelchair. While he was taking Luke to the car, I stopped by the nurses' station and asked about his allergic reaction. He'd be fine, they assured me. I hoped they knew what they were talking about.

"Aren't we going up on the mountain?" Luke asked as I turned onto the Birmingham highway.

"We're coming back tomorrow, all four of us. You, me, Richard, and Mary Alice. I think I can get a key for the house and we can look around in there and in the church, too. Maybe the woman who has the key can tell us some people to talk to, too."

"They'll all be gone to West Virginia."

"Surely not all of them."

Luke sighed. He was sitting very straight and holding the plastic bag in his lap. Which I was grateful for.

"Richard told me all that happened to the Crawford guy. God, I can't believe it."

"It was awful," I agreed.

"And in Virginia's car. Can you believe it?"

I couldn't.

"Well, at least it's got a leather interior."

"Lucky."

It was a beautiful day and Luke didn't seem to be turning paler or green.

"Does your head still hurt?" I asked him.

"Only if I move."

"Well, I'm going to take you to Mary Alice's and get you settled. Okay?"

"Fine."

"You're welcome to come to my house, but Richard's staying with her and they're expecting you up there."

"Fine."

"She's got all the room in the world, you know." I didn't know why I was babbling. "But you're welcome to come to my house."

"Mary Alice's is fine."

I slowed down behind a pickup truck with a Confederate flag decal across the back window.

"This lady who probably has the key is the girl we found in the church's sister. Looks just like her. She told me she was sure Virginia was all right, that Holden Crawford was a kind man."

"Good." Luke clutched the plastic bag and gazed out at the mountains and valleys that we were moving through slowly because of Mr. Confederate in front of us and a curvy road that made passing impossible.

"You know, Patricia Anne, I've been married to that woman for over forty years and I've never messed around with anybody else in all those years except one time at a convention in New Orleans." He sighed. "Well, maybe twice, but the second one was hearsay."

I didn't want to hear this, but he wasn't going to spare me.

"We had our ups and downs, but who

145

doesn't? Did I say one word to that woman when she did the hootchie-kootchie at the club that New Year's Eve?" Another sigh. "She did stuff like that, Patricia Anne. Stuff like the hootchie-kootchie."

The hootchie-kootchie? Best not ask. Carmen Miranda, Charo, and bananas came to mind.

The streaks across Luke's cheeks were turning a bright red. I tried to change the subject.

"Maybe tomorrow you'll feel like going to see Debbie's new baby. He's precious. They're going to call him Brother."

It didn't work.

"I ought to just tell that Crawford guy 'Here she is and welcome to her.' See how he likes it when she starts hootchie-kootchying up there in his church."

"He's dead, Luke," I reminded him.

"That's beside the point. The point, Patricia Anne, is that if Virginia wants to sow her wild oats in somebody else's field, then maybe I'll just find another field to sow my own wild oats in."

A little confusion here, but I knew where he was coming from. He was hurt, worried, and angry, but, personally, my sympathies were on Virginia's side of the fence. How many wild oats did one have left to sow at sixty-four? How many hootchie-kootchies?

I passed the pickup and shot the startled driver a bird.

You go, girl.

Chapter Twelve

"Thomas Benson? Sure I know him. He owns the feed store up in Steele. Still shows up most days for work, but his son's running the business now because of Thomas's health problems. Good old fellow."

Virgil Stuckey stretched his legs toward the fire. One more stretch like that and he would be out of the chair and on his butt on the floor.

The six of us, Virgil, Luke, Richard, Sister, Fred, and I were sitting in Sister's den surrounded by dirty dishes and cartons of Chinese takeout. The smell of sweet-and-sour shrimp battled bravely with the giant arrangement of flowers, mostly purple, on the table behind the sofa. Through the glass wall of the adjoining sunporch, we could see the whole city of Birmingham crisscrossed by the yellow-white ribbons that were interstates. Airplanes took off and landed at the airport, flashing lights. And to our left, the giant statue of Vulcan held up a green torch that looked exactly like a huge lime popsicle, green because there had been no traffic deaths within the city limits in the preceding twenty-four hours. A death warrants a cherry popsicle.

Sister had called around five o'clock to say she and Richard were back from Pulaski, that Virgil was with them, and they were ordering Chinese. Did we want some? Since I had spent what was left of the afternoon visiting Debbie and the baby instead of thinking about supper, we certainly did. And it had been a very pleasant supper around the fire.

"Is this Benson guy one of the snake handlers?" Richard asked.

"Most probably," Virgil answered. Which meant that of course he was.

Richard got up and stood with his back to the fire. If he had been a woman in a skirt, he would have hiked it up. As it was, he rubbed his hands up and down his pants leg, absorbing the heat.

"How come you don't arrest them, Sheriff?" he asked.

"That little thing called freedom of religion,

A slight tension entered the air.

"I don't bother them as long as they don't bother or hurt other folks."

"Well, somebody sure as hell bothered Monk Crawford," Richard said.

"And we'll arrest him. Or her."

Mary Alice jumped up from the sofa. "I forgot the fortune cookies."

She went into the kitchen and came back with a small sack. She handed it to me. I was sitting on the floor on a pillow with my head against Fred's leg. I took a cookie for both of us and passed the sack to Luke. He had been very quiet all night and I wondered if he shouldn't be in bed.

"Everybody read them out loud," Mary Alice insisted. "Patricia Anne, you go first."

The slip of paper from my fortune cookie informed me that I would become rich. Fred's said, "You will never die." Luke's read, "Better things are coming."

And then Virgil's.

"You will soon be released from the insane asylum." He burst out laughing.

"What? You're making that up," Sister said.

"I swear that's what it says."

"It does not." Sister grabbed the message from Virgil.

"You will soon be released from the insane asylum." She looked up, laughing. "Y'all, that's what it really says."

She patted Virgil's hand and, still giggling, said that her fortune cookie advised, "Befriend yourself as a child," whatever that meant.

And then we all looked at Richard who still stood before the fire.

"You will marry Miss America," he said sheepishly and threw the paper into the fire.

"Hey, that may be better than not dying, Richard," Fred laughed.

"No way. Those women have all those make-the-world-a-better-place causes. And every one of them has breast implants."

"He knows," Luke spoke up. "He dated a Miss Mississippi for several months. Whatever happened to that girl, Richard?"

"She was out in Washington hugging trees last I heard." He stretched. "I'm tired. I think I'll call it a day."

"Me, too." Luke stood up and swayed a little. Virgil reached out and steadied him.

"What time tomorrow, Patricia Anne?"

"Whenever you're ready, Luke. And only if you feel like it. I talked to Betsy Mahall about the key and she said she'd be home all day."

"Okay. Good night, y'all."

"Good night," Richard added.

"Did something happen today that I don't know about?" I asked after they had gone upstairs. "Richard seems antsy."

Virgil explained. "Virginia was in the car with Monk Crawford when they got to Pulaski. There was a receipt on the floor from a gas station not far from where he was found. Virginia had signed it. When he checked and showed them her picture, they remembered her."

My arm clasped Fred's leg.

"Which means?" Surely they didn't believe Virginia had been involved in Monk's death.

"We don't know," Virgil admitted. "All we know is that she was in Pulaski and that the guy she was with is dead."

"Snakebit," Fred said. His hand was on my head and I felt his fingers tighten. "Shit."

And then what I knew was coming.

"I really don't want you involved in this, Patricia Anne. It's too dangerous. And you're sure as hell not going to find Virginia. Not in Steele."

"Which reminds me," Virgil said. He reached in his pocket and pulled out a cameo on a long gold chain. "This was in Mrs. Nelson's car, between the seats. I meant to give it to Mr. Nelson."

"I don't think that's Virginia's, Virgil. I'll bet that's the cameo that Betsy Mahall was looking for."

I got up, took the cameo, and held it to the light. The profile of a beautiful young woman with her hair pulled back in an old-fashioned bun was carved into a pale pink oval of stone and surrounded by a quarter-inch rim of gold. It was old and exquisite.

"Do you remember Virginia having this?" I asked Sister.

"I don't know anything about Virginia's jewelry." Sister reached over Virgil, took the cameo, and examined it. "This doesn't look like her, though." And to Virgil, "She's the diamond tennis bracelet type."

"It's got to be Susan Crawford's, Mary Alice. The one Betsy was asking about."

"What about it?" Virgil wanted to know.

"She wondered if we'd seen a cameo when we found her sister's body," I explained. "She said that Susan wore it all the time, but they hadn't given it to her when they gave her Susan's effects."

"Let me see that," Fred said.

Mary Alice passed it over to him.

"My grandmother used to have one of these. Everybody's grandmother did. Why don't I just go ask Luke if it's Virginia's?"

"It's not," I said. I knew in my bones that this was the cameo that had belonged to Susan Crawford.

"Guess I'd better keep it, then," Virgil said when Fred came back with the news that neither Luke nor Richard had recognized the cameo.

He put it back in his pocket.

"No use telling anybody about it yet." He looked right at me. "Okay?"

151

"Okay."

"You better make her cross her heart and hope to die," Sister said. "She can't keep a secret two minutes. Never has been able to."

"Pot calling the kettle black."

Virgil smiled. "Cross your heart, Patricia Anne. You too, Mary Alice."

"You don't have to worry about me, Virgil," Sister said. "I'm always discreet." Then, "Quit laughing, Fred."

"Sorry." He reached over, took my hands, and pulled me up. "We'd better call it a night, oh, sister of the discreet one."

"I need to help Sister clean up."

"I'll help her," Virgil offered.

We said our goodnights and thank-yous and headed home. We both agreed that we liked Virgil. Fred even went so far as to say Mary Alice might have found herself a winner this time. He also warned me again not to get involved with this "snake-handling foolishness."

"Dangerous as hell, honey."

I agreed.

It was a clear, cold night. A full moon was rising over Red Mountain, a moon as pink and delicate as a cameo.

It was the first night since we had gotten back from Warsaw that I had had trouble sleeping. I finally gave up, went into the den, snuggled under the afghan, and tried to read. But even the new Carolyn Hart mystery couldn't take my mind off of everything that had happened in the last few days.

I thought about Richard asking if there

could have been a few minutes outside the church while Mary Alice and I had been waiting for Luke, a few minutes when we hadn't been paying attention. Long enough for someone to have attacked Luke and then darted to the house or hidden behind one of the rocks.

Probably so, I decided.

Or they could have run out the side as we opened the front door looking for Luke. Had I called his name as I pushed open the door? I couldn't remember, but it was possible. That would have warned them. Or they could have ducked behind one of the pews and slipped out the front during the confusion while Mary Alice and I were discovering a bleeding Luke and a dead Susan Crawford.

A Susan Crawford placed on the bench as if she were lying in state. A Susan Crawford who might have been killed in the church, but who had red clay on her boots. Which could mean nothing. The soil on Chandler Mountain wasn't red clay, but it's common enough in most parts of north Alabama. She could have gotten it on her boots walking in her own front yard, for all I knew.

I sighed and turned on my side. Muffin jumped up beside me, purring, happy for night company. I stroked her and felt a slight crackle of electricity.

What, I thought, if the murderer had been placing Susan's body on the bench when Luke entered the church. He could have ducked behind the box the snakes were kept in, and when Luke saw Susan and started

153

toward her, he could have tried to run out of the side door. Luke could have turned and seen—

Virginia.

But why?

He had to be mistaken. Even if there were a reason for Virginia to want Susan dead, there was no way she could have broken her neck, twisted it around. Virginia was a woman in her sixties and no Amazon.

Unless it were an accident. Was that possible? A fall on the rocks? If so, why not just call 911? Why lay her out so symbolically in the church, her hands folded. Besides, Virginia couldn't have picked Susan's body up, let alone carry it any distance.

But there had to be some connection between Susan's death and Monk's. The cameo. Had Susan been in the car? Been killed in the car, the cameo slipping off as her neck was broken? Were the snakes that would mean death to Monk Crawford already in the car when he and Virginia drove to Pulaski?

And how in the hell had Virginia Nelson gotten mixed up in this anyway?

E-MAIL
FROM: HALEY
TO: MAMA AND PAPA
SUBJECT: THE POPE

You will never believe this. Philip and I are going to Rome this weekend for an audience with the pope. I swear, y'all. Isn't that the most wonderful thing you ever heard of? It's not going to be one of those stand in a crowd things where he waves and blesses everybody at one time, either. This is going to be a sure-enough face-to-face, how-do-you-do, bless-you-my-child handshake, or whatever he does, meeting.

So we're off to meet the pope. What do you think I should wear? Ask Aunt Sister. She knows about stuff like that. I know I'm supposed to cover my head. But are you supposed to bow? Don't you kiss his ring or something?

I don't speak Polish well enough to ask anybody here. Don't want them to know I'm so naive anyway. Call down at St. Paul's, Mama, and see what they say. Philip is laughing about it. Because I'm so nervous and excited. But imagine being blessed by the pope himself. And I think Philip is a lot more excited than he's letting on.

Aren't the Trimms across the street Catholic? And Celia, Freddie's girlfriend? They probably wouldn't know, though. This is sure enough big time. Maybe you'd better call St. Paul's.

Let me know as soon as you can. We're leaving day after tomorrow.

I love you both,
   Haley

"Fred," I called, "come look at this E-mail from Haley. It's wonderful."

He came in, buttoning his shirt. I moved

out of the chair so he could sit in front of the computer, but I leaned over him while he read.

"Can you believe that?" I asked when I thought he had had time to get the gist of the message.

He scrolled down. "She sounds excited."

"Of course she's excited, Fred. They're going to be blessed by the pope. Isn't that wonderful?"

"But Haley's a Protestant, and Philip's Jewish."

"Damn it, Fred. It's the pope." I reached down and unplugged the computer. "Go to work."

"Why? What's the matter, honey?"

"You," I said, pointing, "are as blank as that computer screen. Just go to work."

"What's wrong with you, Patricia Anne?"

But he was talking to my back. I went into the bedroom and shut the door. Hard. How had the two of us, as different as we were, managed to live together in relative peace for over forty years?

"Because you adore each other," Mitzi Phizer said a half-hour later when I posed the question to her. She had seen me going through the gate with Woofer and called for me to wait, that she wanted to walk with us. "He's your anchor, and you're his imagination."

"But the pope, Mitzi! Can you imagine anybody not being excited about meeting the pope?"

Mitzi laughed. And then like Sophia on *The Golden Girls,* said, "Picture this. The Vatican, 2001. Two old ladies from Alabama stand in the crowd for hours. The door to a balcony opens. A figure dressed in white, the pope, steps out, waves to the crowd. The women feel faint; they are blessed, ecstatic. They float back to their hotel, where their husbands say, yes, they just watched it on TV. The pope must have cut himself shaving. He had a Band-Aid on his chin."

I giggled. "That's exactly what Fred and Arthur would do, isn't it?"

"Absolutely. And then they would take us somewhere great for lunch."

"So we'd come out ahead any way you look at it."

"The way I look at it, we would."

We stopped for Woofer to mark a telephone pole.

"How's Luke?" Mitzi asked. "Did you have any trouble getting him home yesterday?"

"No. He was still pretty weak last night, though. We're supposed to go up to Steele today to look in Holden Crawford's house to see if we can find any clues as to Virginia's whereabouts."

"Any recent developments?"

It was amazing how much had happened that I hadn't told Mitzi. Four blocks worth of talking. And that didn't include the cameo.

As we stopped in front of her driveway, Mitzi shook her head.

"I don't know, Patricia Anne. This whole

thing just scares the hell out of me. Snakes. Lord." She held out a gloved hand and touched my arm. "Y'all be careful."

"We will."

It seemed like such a small thing to promise. Of course we would be careful. I thanked her for the Vatican story, for putting me in a better mood, went in my gate and checked Woofer's water. A small rim of ice had formed around the side of the bowl during the night. But it was going to be a beautiful January day. I took his leash off and went inside to call Sister and E-mail Haley.

E-MAIL
FROM: MAMA
TO: HALEY
SUBJECT: THE POPE

Darling,

How wonderful. What an opportunity. I haven't called St. Paul's yet, but here's what your Aunt Sister says. Lord only knows where she learns these things, but she's probably right. A dark suit, a handkerchief on your head, not a necessity since you aren't Catholic but you'll probably feel more comfortable. No bow, no ring kissing. He'll probably just take your hand in his, no shake, and you say your name, or if someone has introduced you, "How do you do, Your Holiness." (This doesn't sound right. I'll check it out. I doubt Sister knows diddly about this part.)

The pope. Imagine. Sometimes I wish the

Methodists had a pope, and robes and incense and chants and intercessions and infallible people. I think.

I love you,
Mama

Chapter Thirteen

Betsy Mahall had given me directions to her house. Turn left on Three Fork Road, third driveway on the right. We'd see the name on the mailbox.

"I think we've missed it," Mary Alice said after we had passed two mailboxes and gone at least half a mile. We were in her Jaguar, just the two of us. I wasn't sure how she managed it. But when she blew the horn and I went out, got in the car, and asked where Richard and Luke were, she said, "Don't ask. They're meeting us on the mountain at 1:00."

"Is Luke okay this morning?" I asked.

"He ate three poached eggs and half a pound of bacon for breakfast. You think I was going to let him in my car?"

So Sister and I had made the trip to Steele by ourselves. It was nice to have someone to talk to who was excited as I was about Haley and the pope.

"I almost got to meet him," Sister said.

"Roger was Catholic, remember?" (Actually, I didn't. But who could keep up?) "And he was saying on the plane right before he died, you know, when we were coming back from Europe, that the next time we went he was going to arrange for an audience with the pope, that he should have done it this time." She paused. "I guess maybe his chest hurting made him think of it."

A red pickup truck passed us. The driver waved and we waved back.

"And not a single priest on that plane," Sister continued. "There we were, halfway across the Atlantic and Roger turning blue and not a single priest. Some nun, said she was a nun, anyway, didn't even have on nun clothes, just a red knit dress, read him his last rites."

"That was Terry Mahall," I said.

"You know who the nun was?"

"The guy in the red truck that just passed. That was Betsy's husband. We're not lost."

"Oh. Well, they sure as hell live out in the woods," Sister grumbled.

Actually Three Fork Road wound through a valley below Chandler Mountain, a valley that was lying fallow in January, but that was crisscrossed with fields that had yielded a harvest in the fall. Dead stalky plants marching down rows attested to that. Cotton? Soy beans? Any woods that might have been here once were only a memory. This was farm country.

"There's a mailbox," I pointed.

Mary Alice slowed down and we turned onto an asphalt driveway, a long driveway that led to a beautiful, large house, the type of house that Mary Alice has always wanted, a Tara with six columns across the front. The driveway circled around a grassy area that had in its center a fountain (a voluptuous woman pouring water from a jug into a small pool) encircled by pansies.

"This has got to be the wrong place," I said. "This isn't somebody who works for the telephone company's house unless he's the CEO."

"It said Mahall on the mailbox." Sister pointed. "Look at those columns, Mouse. Those aren't that drivet stuff. I think this is a sure-enough antebellum house. One the Yankees missed."

"It's money's what it is. And I don't think it belongs to Betsy and Terry. But I'll see."

"See if whoever lives there will let us in, anyway," Sister said as I got out. "I want to see the inside. I'll bet it's got those wonderful old Thomas Jefferson floors. You know, like at Monticello."

I had no idea in the world what she was talking about. Thomas Jefferson floors? But the house was certainly impressive. I crossed a short brick walkway, stepped up two steps to the red-tile porch that stretched the width of the house, and rang the doorbell. I heard the familiar "Avon calling" chime, and a dog began to bark shrilly. I also heard a man's voice say, "Hush," I assumed to the dog.

I shook my head at Mary Alice. Wrong house. It had to be.

The door opened, and an elderly man in a

wheelchair looked up at me. He was wearing a pale blue sweater that matched his eyes, a faded blue. A small terrier sat in his lap, teeth bared.

"Yes?"

The man looked like Colonel Sanders, white hair, goatee. For a second I wondered if this is what happens when you get older, you've seen so many faces that they all begin to resemble each other, like Virgil Stuckey and Willard Scott. That maybe there are only so many faces to go around.

"Yes?" he asked again.

"Is this the Mahall residence?"

"I'm Eugene Mahall."

"Does Betsy Mahall live here?"

"I sure do." Betsy came down the steps into the wide hall. "Mrs. Hollowell, this is my father-in-law, Eugene Mahall."

"I told her who I was," the old man said.

Betsy reached in her jeans pocket and handed me a key.

"Mrs. Hollowell is going up to Monk's house," she explained to her father-in-law.

"What for?" he asked. He and the dog both looked at me suspiciously.

"They're trying to find her cousin."

"Bunch of fools up there." Mr. Mahall whirled his chair around and disappeared into the room on the left. The dog gave a bark.

Betsy stepped out onto the porch. "Do be careful," she said.

The key was in my hand and I considered giving it back. "We're not going to find any snakes up there, are we?"

162

Betsy shook her head. "No. Terry and I were up there yesterday after the funeral looking for the cameo one more time. All's clear."

I had to bite my tongue to keep from telling her the cameo had been found. As it was, I told her I was sure it would turn up soon.

"I'm still hoping," she said. "I'd go with you today, but I have to stay with the children."

"Are they okay?"

"They're fine. Ethan's napping and Jamie's watching Mr. Rogers."

"And you?"

"I'm all right. Yesterday was rough."

"Betsy?" her father-in-law called.

"I'm sorry, Mrs. Hollowell. I'd ask you in, but things are sort of in a mess right now."

"That's fine, Betsy." I held up the key. "We'll get this back to you later this afternoon."

"No problem. I doubt I'll be going up there anytime soon."

"Betsy!" The call was a command.

"I've got to go, Mrs. Hollowell." She gave me an apologetic look.

"I'll talk to you later."

By the time I'd crossed the porch, I heard the door closing.

"What was that about?" Sister wanted to know. "Who was the old guy?"

"Her father-in-law. I may be wrong, but my guess is that this is his house and they live with him. I think Betsy's got her hands full, you ask me."

"Did you see the floors?"

"No, I didn't see the floors."

163

But I had seen enough to know that the version I had had in my mind of the young Mahalls' small-town life, neighbors, ordinary jobs, everything fine except for the lack of children wasn't the truth. Not by a long shot. I admitted as much to Mary Alice.

"You're not like me, Mouse," she said. "You tend to pigeonhole people." Then, as we started up Chandler Mountain, "God, I hope none of those snake handlers are up at the church. They've all got to be crazy as bedbugs."

I ignored this. However crazy handling poisonous snakes might seem to us, I remembered what Betsy had said about her aunt, that she was trying to touch God. That deserved respect.

There were no cars or trucks at the church except Monk Crawford's paint van, which still stood in his driveway. Luke and Richard hadn't gotten there yet.

I held up the key. "You want to go in?"

"Reckon they have a bathroom?"

"I'm sure they do."

"Then I want to go in."

We got out and crossed the gravel walkway between the church and the house. I put the key into the lock and turned it.

"I'll bet the bathroom's where they keep the snakes," I said when I noticed Sister was dancing from one foot to the other.

"Shit, Patricia Anne!"

I moved aside. "Well, go ahead. Just watch your step."

Sister hesitated. "You're just saying that, aren't you?"

Of course I was. But I wasn't entirely comfortable stepping across the threshold.

The ordinariness of the room we entered was reassuring, though. Sun shone across a white vinyl floor. The walls were painted a pale yellow, and the windows were framed with white lace curtains. A green-and-yellow-plaid sofa and two matching chairs in early-American design faced a large TV. Several magazines were arranged neatly on a pine coffee table and brass eagle lamps centered each end table. The brick fireplace had a gas space heater in it, and across the mantel were what appeared to be family photographs.

Sister was reassured enough to go down the hall and yell back, "I found it, and it looks all right."

It was freezing in the house. There was a package of matches on the mantel advertising the Homestead Inn in Nashville. I took it and squatted down to light the space heater, something I hadn't done in a long time. I turned on the gas cautiously, held the match to the heater, and Pow!, I was sitting on my butt with my heart racing. Damn dangerous things. Made you appreciate central heating.

I scrambled up and replaced the matches beside a wedding picture, a thin young groom with a lock of dark hair falling across his forehead (I swear he looked like James Dean). He was wearing a black tux at least two sizes too large and, arm around his bride's waist, he was looking down lovingly at her, a plump girl in a simple white satin wedding gown. On top of her teased blond hair was a circlet of flowers.

Holden "Monk" Crawford and his wife. It had to be. And the other wedding picture was of their son Ethan and his wife Susan. The poses were startlingly similar, with Ethan looking down lovingly at Susan. She had worn her mother-in-law's dress, I realized, a dress that had been scaled down a couple of sizes to fit Susan's smaller body. On her head was an identical circlet of flowers, but it lay against smooth red hair. Ethan's tux was identical to his father's, too. But he was a much larger man and filled it out.

Between these two pictures were smaller ones, family picnics, graduations, Ethan as a child. Ethan holding a baby. Ethan and Susan sitting before a Christmas tree, Susan holding a baby and Ethan with a toddler in his lap.

Mary Alice had come up behind me and was looking over my shoulder.

"This is sad," she said.

I nodded.

"Put your hands up," a man's voice demanded.

Our hands shot up into the air.

"What the hell are you doing here?"

"We're friends," Mary Alice stammered. "We come in peace."

A burst of laughter. "We come in peace? You hear that, Mama? These folks been watching too many of those *Dances with Wolves* movies."

We turned around cautiously to see a large

bearded man dressed in overalls and a denim jacket. On his head was a ratty brown felt hat. Beside him was the ancient woman I had seen on TV, the woman who had been dipping snuff.

"You can put your arms down," she said, still laughing. "Bertie's teasing you." She waddled arthritically over to a chair, bent her knees, and fell more than sat. "But just what the hell *are* you doing here?"

We looked at Bertie. He nodded, and we put our hands down.

"Sorry I don't have a peace pipe," he grinned.

"You hush, Bertie," his mother said. "Let them answer."

Sister and I looked at each other. I answered.

"We're looking for our cousin's wife. She was here a few days ago with Mr. Crawford, and we were hoping we could find something that would help us locate her. An address or something." I shrugged. "I don't know what we thought we might find, to tell the truth."

"She an old skinny blond woman with pretty teeth?" the woman asked.

"Caps," Mary Alice said. "All caps."

"Well, they look good. Real white. I bet they cost a lot."

"They did."

"Y'all sit down on the sofa. Bertie, get me some water. It's pill time."

"No, it's not, Mama. You just took them."

"Well, that's why I'm so thirsty then."

We sat on the sofa as we had been instructed to.

167

"I'm Mary Alice Crane," Sister said. "And this is my sister, Patricia Anne Hollowell."

The woman nodded. "Beulah Packard. And that's Bertie."

"Albert Lee, ladies. How do you do," her son called from the kitchen. In a moment he was back with a glass of water, which he handed to his mother.

"Thank you, baby boy," she said.

Baby Boy appeared to be in his early fifties. His beard was liberally streaked with gray. But I adjusted his age down when he sat in the chair opposite his mother and pulled off the disreputable brown felt hat. His hair was thick and dark. He ran his hands through it, propped his hat on his knee, and looked at us.

"Well?" he asked.

"Well, what?" Mary Alice was getting her composure back.

"You do know what's been going on around here, don't you?"

"We're the ones who found Susan Crawford's body, if that's what you mean," I admitted. I looked from the son to the mother. "You're neighbors?"

Beulah Packard nodded. "Live right up the road by Horse Pens. Born and raised right here on Chandler Mountain."

"Not much happens up here Mama doesn't know."

Beulah Packard frowned at her son. "I didn't know Susan was lying over there in that church dead. Bless her heart. Her and Monk both gone." She put her glass beside her chair. "I've got the cat. Guess I'll keep her."

We must have looked puzzled.

"Monk's cat. I keep it for him when he's gone. He brought it up last Friday, I think it was. Said he was going to be gone a couple of days. They were in that old lady with the white teeth's car. She was driving."

"Did he say where they were going?" I asked, thinking this might be the answer to our questions about Virginia.

She shook her head. "Just handed me Flossie and said. 'Miss Beulah, I'll be back in a couple of days. You take good care of my Flossie and keep an eye on my house.' "

She reached in her coat pocket for a Kleenex. "He did love that cat. Lord, I'm going to miss that boy. There was no reason in the world for anybody to do what they did to him."

"Are you members of his church?" Sister wanted to know.

"Dear Jesus, no." Miss Beulah wiped her eyes. "I'm scared as hell of snakes. Worst whipping Bertie ever got was when he put a green snake down in my laundry pile. I like to have died."

"So did I," Bertie said. "And I was sixteen years old."

"Just meanness. Meanest thing you ever did."

The two of them smiled at each other.

"Bertie teaches English at the university," his mother told us. "Monk sort of took his place, cut my grass, helped me plant my garden."

Miss Beulah held the Kleenex to her eyes. Mary Alice and I both looked at the mountain man on our right who was smiling at us. A teacher at the university?

"It's the January short term," he said, as if that explained his appearance. "I don't have any classes until February."

"My sister is an English teacher," Mary Alice pointed to me.

"Oh?" Albert leaned forward. "What's your specialty?"

Specialty? Smart aleck. His mother should have whipped him harder when he was sixteen.

"Eleventh grade, but I'm retired. What's yours?"

"Chaucer. Every one of those people is right here on Chandler Mountain."

I looked around at the four of us and had to grin. He was right. There were questions that needed asking, though.

"How long was our cousin here, Mrs. Packard? Do you know?"

"Couple of days, far as I know. Monk was always bringing women home from his painting jobs. Rescuing them, he said. Bless his heart."

"Do you know the names of any of the other women?"

"Sally Jo was one of them. I don't know her last name, but I remember last summer she came and picked some okra at my house. Said she fried it some kind of special way and she'd give me the recipe. But I think she left the next day. Never got the recipe." Miss Beulah reached down, picked up her glass and held it out to Albert who got up and took it to the kitchen. "None of them stayed more than a couple of days."

"Did any of their husbands show up looking for them?"

"Probably. I never heard of any trouble, though."

Albert Lee came back and handed his mother her water.

"I think Monk was running an underground railroad for unhappy wives," he said.

"Could one of their husbands have hated him enough to kill him?" I asked.

Albert Lee Packard shrugged. "Possibly. I'm assuming Susan and Monk's deaths are connected, though, and there wouldn't have been any reason for a cuckolded husband to have killed her."

"Bertie was in love with Susan," his mother said.

"Everybody was in love with Susan, Mama." He sat down and cracked his knuckles. "Her and those damn snakes." There was such a bitter tone to the last remark, that I realized he probably had cared deeply for Susan.

"The snakes are the connection, ladies," he continued.

His mother shook her head. "But Monk had quit handling."

"Which would have been seen as a loss of faith, Mama. Suppose someone was furious at him because of that. What more symbolic way to kill him than to stick his arm into a basket of snakes?"

Mary Alice had been unusually quiet. Now she shuddered and said, "It gives me the chills to think about it."

"I still think it could have been the Chandler Mountain booger broke Susan's neck," Miss Beulah said.

171

We heard noises outside, car doors slamming.

"That must be my cousin," I said. I stood up to look. But a car and a pickup had pulled up in front of the church. Several people were getting out and going in.

Albert had stood up, too. "Probably getting ready for Monk's funeral," he said.

"Did you go to Susan's yesterday?"

"No. It was just a family graveside service."

"Do you know her sister?"

"Sure. Betsy and Terry are good folks."

"That's more than you can say for that father of his," Miss Beulah said. "Eugene Mahall is the biggest ass in St. Clair County. In a wheelchair because somebody shot him. Bunch of people claimed they did it. Bragged about it. The sheriff just gave up on it."

The mention of the sheriff got Mary Alice's attention. "Virgil Stuckey?"

"Good man. Not worth a tinker's damn as a sheriff, though."

"Oh?" I could see Mary Alice bristling.

"Too nice." Miss Beulah struggled to get up from the chair. Albert went over to help her.

"We've got to go," she said. "I've got a pot of vegetable soup on. Y'all are welcome to come by and have some. The green house right on the road. Still got collards in the garden."

We thanked her but said we didn't know how long we would be at the house.

As they started out of the door, she turned and said, "I've got Monk's mail. I pick it up for him when he's out of town, so I've been getting it. Y'all can look at it if you want to. There might be a letter from your cousin or something. I know there's a phone bill."

"Mama, you'd better give that to the sheriff," Albert cautioned.

"Shoot. He wouldn't know what to do with it."

"Old fool," Sister muttered as I closed the door. "You think that son of hers really teaches at the university?"

"Probably." I turned around and surveyed the room. "Reckon how much nosying around we can do without getting in trouble?"

"Betsy gave you the key, didn't she? And I guess Virgil's through in here. Why?"

"Just wondered."

Actually, Miss Beulah's mention of the telephone bill had reminded me that there might be phone messages. I went into the kitchen where a telephone was on the counter and picked up the receiver. I recognized the rhythmic beep that Bellsouth uses to signify messages. It's the same answering service I have at home. Unfortunately, it requires a number that varies for each area as well as a number-password. The number we use is Fred's birthday, which wouldn't help me much here.

"Damn," I said. "He's got messages, but he's on Bellsouth."

Sister had followed me into the kitchen.

"I'm sure Virgil's already checked them."

I ignored the smugness. "These are new ones," I explained. "It doesn't beep unless there are new ones. Virgil could have saved the old ones, but they'd just be sitting there."

"You can't access them?"

"Not without the code numbers."

"Hmm." Mary Alice started opening kitchen cabinets.

"What are you doing?"

"We're supposed to be looking, aren't we?" She took down an opened package of Oreos. "Reckon these are fresh? Remember that time you bit into one of those wafer cookies with the lard stuff in them and there was half a worm hanging out when you started to take your second bite?"

I remembered that it was a cookie that she had given me not mentioning that it was old as the hills.

"I'm sure those Oreos are fine," I said, praying for a worm.

No such luck.

"Let's see what they've got to drink," Sister said, opening the refrigerator, her mouth full.

"Apple juice is all. You want some?"

I shook my head no. I had opened the drawer beside the sink that is everyone's junk drawer. On top were a couple of matchbooks like the one on the mantel advertising the Homestead Inn in Nashville. I pocketed one of them. It had the inn's phone number on it. Could Monk and Virginia have been there and on their way back through Pulaski when he was killed?

No, that didn't make sense. That way the matchbooks would have ended up in Pulaski, not on Chandler Mountain. Nevertheless, someone had been to the Homestead Inn.

"Hello?" The front door opened and Terry Mahall stepped inside.

"I'm Terry Mahall," he reminded us politely. "Betsy sent me to see if I could help you."

"You can tell us what we're looking for," Mary Alice said. "We sure don't know."

"Can't help you there, Mrs.—"

"Crane."

I closed the junk drawer and walked into the living room. Terry was a handsome young man, I realized. I recognized his father's pale blue eyes.

"I'm Patricia Anne Hollowell, Terry," I said, "and my sister's right. We're not sure what we're looking for. Something that will tell us what might have happened to our cousin."

I glanced out of the window. There were several more cars and pickups parked between the house and church than there had been just a few minutes earlier.

Terry followed my glance.

"They're gathering," he said.

"They?"

"The handlers. They'll all be here for Monk's funeral. Far away as West Virginia."

Sister had joined us. "Will they have snakes?"

Terry shrugged. "It's winter. I don't know."

There was a knock on the door and we all jumped. Richard stuck his head inside.

"Just checking. Sorry we're late, but Daddy got sick a couple of times on the way up here. Had to stop at a Grub-mart for some Pepto-Bismol."

He turned and called, "They're here okay, Daddy. Come on in."

"Dear Jesus," Mary Alice said. "Maybe he ought to wait out in the car."

"Too cold." Richard went to help his father.

Mary Alice turned to me. "What the hell are we doing here?"

Damned if I knew.

Chapter Fourteen

An hour later, the four of us, Richard, Luke, Mary Alice, and I, were back in the living room with nothing to show for our search. Terry Mahall had left right after Richard and Luke had arrived. But before he left, he had called Betsy to ask if she knew how to get messages from Monk's telephone. She didn't know, but said she would try to find out. So far we hadn't heard from her.

Luke was lying on the sofa, Sister and I were sitting in the chairs, and Richard was standing by the fireplace looking at the pictures on the mantel. Outside, several more cars had come up, and we could hear people greeting each other. Richard had gone over earlier, introduced himself, and explained that we were looking for his mother. None of them said they had met her or knew anything about her. He had come back to report that they were decorating the church with pine boughs and little lights as if it were Christmas. And no, he answered Sister's question, he hadn't seen any snakes.

"We might as well go," he said, turning from the mantel. Tears suddenly filled his eyes. "She's dead, isn't she?"

None of us answered.

Richard walked over to the sofa and stared down at Luke. "What the hell did you do to her, Daddy?"

Luke sat up. "What do you mean, what the hell did I do to her? Fed her and put a house over her head for forty years, is what I did to her."

"Well, that answers that," Richard said. "No wonder she left."

"Hey, y'all, this is tacky." Mary Alice stood up. "Come on. Richard's right. It's time to go."

But Luke wasn't to be sidetracked.

"What the hell do you know about marriage, you ungrateful punk. You and your Miss Boobie Bungalow. Think you're so high and mighty up there running the whole United States. Well, I've got some news for you, sonny boy."

"I'm turning off the gas," I said, jumping up. "Y'all act the fool all you want, but close the door good when you leave."

They were glaring at each other when Sister and I grabbed our coats and left.

"Tacky," she repeated as we stepped out onto the porch. "Common as pig tracks. What do you suppose brought that on?"

"They're just tired and worried. They'll be crying and hugging in a little while."

"I hope so."

So did I.

We both realized at the same time that there was no way that we could leave. The Jaguar was blocked by two pickups and a shiny black Studebaker with ANTIQUE CAR on the tag.

"Would you look at that," Sister said admiringly. "That's the kind of car I had before Will Alec and I got married. Remember? I got it real cheap because it smelled so bad. I think a cat died in it or something. It was okay with the windows down, though."

She walked over and looked in the car. "This is great. I wonder if they want to sell it."

"Maybe they'll swap with you."

"You ladies need something?" A man in overalls and a plaid flannel shirt had come from the church and was walking toward us.

Sister pointed to the multiple vehicles behind us. "We're blocked in."

"You sure are," the man agreed. He took off an Atlanta Braves cap and ran his hand through thinning gray hair. "I'll see can I find out who these trucks belong to. The Studebaker's mine."

"It's beautiful. I used to have one like it," Mary Alice said.

"Good for you." He held out his hand. "Joe Baker. Monk's brother-in-law."

We shook hands. He was a thin, frail-looking man in his sixties, but his grip was so strong it hurt.

"You find everything all right in the house? My sister always kept it neat as a pin. I don't know since she died though, and Monk's been bringing all these women in."

"The house is fine," I said.

Joe Baker frowned as if he doubted that seriously. Then he said, "Your boy told us what you were doing, trying to locate his mama."

"We are."

"Well, could be she's in Nashville. That's where Monk was going Friday. I talked to him Thursday night. Said he had a painting job up there."

"But he was found dead in her car in Pulaski," Sister said.

Joe Baker shrugged. "Don't know." Then, "I'll see whose trucks these are."

I reached in my pocket, pulled out the Heritage Inn matchbook, and handed it to Sister.

"There were a bunch of these in the house. Maybe this is where he usually stayed when he had a job in Nashville."

She shook her head. "Sounds too fancy. I think we need to tell Virgil about it, though."

Two men accompanied Joe Baker from the church, nodded to us, and got in their pickups.

"Sorry." He waved.

In a few minutes we were on the road and headed toward the crest of the mountain. When we got to the green house that Mrs. Packard had described, Mary Alice surprised me by pulling into the driveway.

"What?" I asked.

"I want to find out if she knew Monk was going to Nashville so I can tell Virgil."

179

"And we might as well eat some soup while we're here."

Sister didn't hesitate. "Might as well."

Albert Packard answered the door with a copy of *Ulysses* in his hand. I was sure he had grabbed it when he saw us through the window. I was still impressed, though.

"Well, ladies. You're just in time. Mama's just taking the cornbread out."

Books were everywhere. They were in bookcases along the walls, stacked in piles on the floor as well as every other surface. The only piece of furniture that didn't have books on it was the rocking chair I recognized from TV, the one Miss Beulah had been sitting in when they interviewed her.

"Have you read all these?" Sister asked in amazement.

"I've forgotten. Y'all come on in."

We followed him through a path of books toward a sofa.

"Mama," Albert called, "Mrs. Hollowell and Mrs. Crane are here."

"Okay, baby boy."

Baby Boy moved some books to the floor and picked up a large orange tabby. The cat hung lazily over his arm. "Y'all have a seat."

We did, squeezing together. Some books slid into Sister's lap.

"Sorry," Baby Boy said, putting the cat down and taking the books from Sister.

I looked around for two things, a fire extinguisher and the tin can that Miss Beulah spit her snuff in. Neither was in evidence.

"I know this looks like a mess." Albert

swept his hand in a wave around the room. "But I'm an antiquarian."

"Well, none of us is getting any younger," Sister commiserated.

"He collects books," I explained.

Another book fell into her lap. "Well, that's obvious."

"God's truth." Miss Beulah stood in the arched entrance to the dining room where more books were stacked on the table. "Can't breathe in here for dust mites."

"Now, Mama." Albert Lee smiled. "What's happened," he explained to us, "is that I've had this little store in Tuscaloosa for years dealing in rare books and first editions, and I've decided to close it and go on the Internet. No use paying the rent. Most of the business is done on the net, anyway."

I picked up the book on the top of the pile next to me. A first edition signed copy of *The Great Santini* by Pat Conroy. I actually felt goosebumps. I had wandered into book heaven right here on the top of Chandler Mountain. Snake handlers and rare-book dealers. What a strange combination.

"I've got to find a place to store them," Albert Lee admitted.

"God's truth," Miss Beulah said again. Then, "Y'all want some vegetable soup and cornbread? I promise there's not even a cookbook in the kitchen."

Mary Alice didn't hesitate. I think she beat Miss Beulah back into the kitchen. I wasn't quite as fast.

Albert Lee was perceptive. "You admiring

181

the books or did you see Mama on TV the other night?"

"Both," I admitted.

He laughed. "She loves to do that. She's even got one of those old sunbonnets and a long dress she wears when they're having a festival at Horse Pens. Hangs Aunt Beulah's handmade quilts out on the porch. Causes fender benders sometimes people stopping so quick to pay a fortune for them."

"She makes quilts?"

"Somebody in the Dominican Republic does."

"Well, my goodness."

"Come eat some soup," he said kindly.

A round oak table was set with different colors of Fiesta ware on quilted placemats. In the middle was a tureen shaped like a rooster and on an orange Fiesta platter a large pone of steaming cornbread was already cut. The whole scene could have been an illustration for *Southern Living*.

Albert Lee lifted the head from the chicken. "Pass me your bowls."

And we did. The next few minutes were spent concentrating on eating. I looked over at Miss Beulah who was delicately spooning her soup away from her as if she had just graduated from some finishing school.

I was stereotyping her again, I realized, to my shame. Albert Lee caught my glance and smiled.

"Did you find anything at the house?" he asked, passing the platter of cornbread around for seconds.

"Not really." I said. "Some matchbooks from the Homestead Inn in Nashville. But there was a guy with an old Studebaker, Monk's brother-in-law, said that Monk had paint jobs in Nashville. This could have been where he stayed."

Miss Beulah took another piece of cornbread. "A man named Joe Baker?"

"That was who." Mary Alice took another piece of cornbread and passed the plate to me. "I used to have a car like that. Smelled awful, but I loved the way the front and the back looked the same so you couldn't tell if it was coming or going."

"That Joe Baker." Miss Beulah speared her knife into the butter so hard that it clinked against the dish. "Bad news. Probably the one who killed Monk. Susan, too. I wouldn't put it past him."

"Now, Mama," Albert Lee admonished.

"Well, you know it's the truth, Bertie. Killed two of his wives. One of them was snakebit and didn't even handle. And the other one drowned in their well. Just happened to fall over a four-foot-high rock curbing." She slathered butter on her bread. "Sure ruined that water supply."

I passed on the cornbread and handed the plate to Albert Lee.

"But why would he want to kill Monk and Susan?" Mary Alice asked.

"Well," Miss Beulah took a bite of cornbread, chewed, and swallowed. "Monk told me that Joe Baker wanted him to give him his snakes when he quit handling, said he thought he was due them. But Monk gave them to Susan, instead."

I looked down at the *Southern Living* table, at the beautiful, rare books in the next room. There was a surreal quality to this conversation. To this whole place.

"More soup?" Albert Lee offered. Sister held out her bowl.

"Will Joe Baker be the head honcho snake handler now?" she asked.

"I expect so. Up here on Chandler Mountain, anyway," Miss Beulah said.

I remembered how strong Joe Baker's handshake had been. How it had hurt my hand. He could twist someone's head around, force someone's hand into a basket of poisonous snakes. I shook my head when Albert Lee offered me more soup.

"She's anorexic," Sister explained. "Doesn't eat enough to keep a bird alive."

I denied the accusation, but no one was listening to me. Miss Beulah was reciting Joe Baker's criminal record, which was astounding. Several drug charges, federal racketeering (whatever that was), manslaughter (killed a woman while driving drunk). Bunch of other stuff she couldn't remember.

Obviously, in Joe Baker's heyday, the three-strikes-and-you're-out law wasn't in effect.

"Bad news," she repeated. "If I was Virgil Stucky, Joe would be at the top of my list, I guarantee you."

Mary Alice perked up at the mention of Virgil's name and asked Miss Beulah if she knew him very well.

"Nicest man in the world. Needs to get him another wife and settle down."

Mary Alice nodded in heartfelt agreement.

Miss Beulah pointed her spoon toward Albert Lee. "Bertie does, too. Look at that beard. Scraggling down like Spanish moss. No woman in the world would put up with that."

"Patsy left me because I'm gay, Mama."

"Gay, my foot, Albert Lee Packard. She left you because of those damn books in yonder."

Mother and son smiled affectionately at each other. From what she had said about Albert's affection for Susan Crawford, I doubted that he was gay, but saw that whatever he was, his mother adored him.

It was pleasant in the kitchen. Outside, the January wind had picked up, but we were warm and well fed. Albert Lee got up and cut pieces of pecan pie for us for dessert and poured coffee. I ate and listened idly to the conversation, most of it about Chandler Mountain, the crops grown there late into the fall because of the thermals, the hard-core poverty of the Appalachians, the mountain people trying to hold on to their isolation and losing the battle.

"But you left the mountain," I said to Albert Lee.

"Yes, but it's never left me. And here I am, back."

"But on the Internet."

He shrugged and grinned. "There's a world out there."

"And he's going back to it, too," Miss Beulah said. "The day I found out I was pregnant with him was the day I started saving my pennies so he could go to college."

"What did your husband do?" I asked.

"Coal miner." Miss Beulah pushed her coffee cup away. "Died when he was thirty-five in the Daisy Belle mine. Methane explosion. Seventeen men gone just like that." Miss Beulah snapped her finger.

"That was my daddy," Albert Lee said. "There've been a couple of husbands since."

Miss Beulah nodded. "One of them nice but sickly, didn't last long. One of them sorry, wanting the money the company gave me for Jake's death. I kicked his sorry ass out so quick it's probably still spinning."

I wondered how much money she would have received from a coal company forty years ago. Probably not much, but I had an idea that it explained Albert Lee's education.

Mary Alice leaned back and stretched. "How much did you get?"

"Sister!"

But Miss Beulah didn't take offense. "Not as much as I would have if he'd lived. Eugene Mahall down in Steele, Susan Crawford's sister Betsy is married to his son, was hurt in the same accident and he's been living high off the hog from the coal company ever since. Bought a bunch of land, raises cotton, built a fine house."

"Invested it wisely, Mama," Albert Lee said.

Miss Beulah pursed her lips. "So they say. Ask me, he's been blackmailing the company all these years. Probably the folks who shot him. He knew something about the explosion the company's been willing to shut him up about."

"That could have been to start with," Albert Lee agreed. "They could have given him more than they did us. But he took that money and made his own bundle with it, Mama."

"How?" Sister asked. "That's where we picked up the key to Monk's house. That's the prettiest house I've ever seen. The Mahall house, that is."

"Lending money. Charging a fortune in interest." Albert Lee got up and started collecting dirty dishes. "Anybody want any more coffee?"

Nobody did.

"What do they call that? Usury?" Sister asked.

"They call it illegal. He was running a damn mini-Mafia for years. That's how he got shot. Mama knows that." Albert Lee put the dishes into the sink and began to rinse them. "He got away with it, though, and then turned legal. The son of a bitch owns a bank now. He and his son. Lock, stock, and barrel, and the coal company their biggest account."

"You're kidding," I exclaimed. I thought of Betsy Mahall working at the telephone company, of my worry about their being able to afford in-vitro procedures. Was nothing on this damn mountain what it seemed?

"I told you I bet they have Thomas Jefferson floors in that house," Sister said.

"Probably," Miss Beulah agreed as if

Thomas Jefferson floors were common knowledge. "I think that house is why his wife Louellen married the old coot."

"Terry's mother?" I asked.

"No. Terry's mother got taken with pneumonia a long time ago. Louellen was about twenty-five years younger. A country singer. Said she was on the *Grand Ole Opry,* but nobody had ever heard of her. Leastways up here on the mountain, we hadn't. Heard of Conway Twitty, but no Louellen Conway."

Albert Lee sat back down and crossed his arms.

"What's the matter with you?" his mother asked.

"Nothing, Mama. Just waiting to hear the rest of the story."

Miss Beulah gave him a hard look but continued. "Anyway, the girl was cute as she could be, little and blond like Barbara Mandrell, but I think she found out real soon that she'd made a bad bargain."

"I think she was clinically depressed," Albert Lee said.

"Well, of course she was, Bertie. Who wouldn't be, having to live with Eugene Mahall?"

"Did he lose the use of his legs in the explosion?" I asked.

"Sure did. We thought he'd lost more, but then Terry was born, and Terry's mama was a saint, so there wasn't a handyman in the woodpile, I guarantee you."

There was a challenge to Miss Beulah's voice so we all nodded that we were sure that Terry Mahall was indeed a legitimate Mahall.

"Anyway, that Louellen hadn't been there six months until she started trying to commit suicide. Jumped out of a second-story window two times, but just scratched herself up in some legustrum. The third time they say she crawled up on the roof and broke her arm when she jumped."

"Why didn't she just leave him?" Mary Alice asked.

"Well, she did, finally. Just disappeared. Old Eugene Mahall said she went back to Nashville, but everybody thinks she's part of the Welcome to Alabama rest-stop ramp they were building up I-59."

"Lord have mercy," Mary Alice murmured.

The yellow cat strolled into the kitchen and jumped up on Albert's lap.

"Or maybe the Chandler Mountain booger got her," he said, scratching the purring cat's head.

Chapter Fifteen

Mary Alice was unusually quiet on the way home. I don't know what she was thinking about, probably Virgil, but I was thinking about Betsy Mahall and what she had said about being scared. I had tried to make myself believe she was scared about losing the cameo, but what if she were frightened of her father-in-law? Of bringing her sister's two tiny children into that house to live with a man who was at the least disagreeable (I had witnessed that myself) and who, according to the Packards, was a thief, blackmailer, and possibly a murderer.

And what were she and Terry doing living there anyway? Was she running that large house and taking care of a grouchy, disabled father-in-law as well as holding down a job at the telephone company?

"What are you thinking about?" Sister asked.

"Betsy Mahall. I think she's got her hands full. What are you thinking about?"

"I'm thinking that Virginia's no more dead than a Betsy bug. You know what I think happened?"

I didn't ask, but she told me anyway.

"I think Holden Crawford took her to Nashville to that Homestead Inn place and left her. She had arranged to meet someone there."

"Then what was he doing with her car in Pulaski? And somebody saw her with him in Pulaski, remember? Getting gas."

"That could have been on their way up there. On the way back, after he'd left Virginia, somebody killed him."

I thought about this for a minute. It was possible, but certainly a circuitous route for Virginia to get to Nashville. Why would she

190

have come to Chandler Mountain when she could have driven straight up there from Mississippi?

"Or maybe," Sister continued, "he put her on a plane in Nashville."

"Planes fly out of a lot closer places. Birmingham, Chattanooga."

"There was some special reason he needed to go to Nashville."

My head was beginning to ache. I still wasn't over my jet lag totally.

"You want to go with me to Debbie's to see Brother and the twins?"

"Tell her I'll be over tomorrow."

"Maybe Henry's cooked something good for supper."

Lord. It had only been an hour since we had had soup, cornbread, and pecan pie. The woman amazes me. What would it be like to have such an appetite, not just for food, but for life? Not to worry about details like I did? Who made me the worrywart in this family?

"You were born worrying. It's your burden to bear. I remember when Mama told us we should appreciate our food because the starving children in India didn't have any, you worried to death about them. Wouldn't eat."

I hadn't even realized I had asked the question aloud until Sister answered.

"I still worry about them," I admitted. "What's your burden?"

Sister thought for a moment, her eyebrows squeezed together into a crease. "I guess being a woman, particularly a Southern woman."

191

I looked at her in amazement. Surely she wasn't serious. What kind of a burden brought three rich husbands, three wonderful kids, a secure place in the world, and the nerve of a bad tooth?

"You see, we're brought up to be too sweet, too subservient to men, to society in general."

"When on God's earth have you ever been subservient to anybody? Or sweet, for that matter? On the Concorde coming back from Paris, you rearranged where half a dozen people were sitting so you could be near Peter Jennings."

"Who slept the whole way home. And I was sweet and didn't wake him up. He's got a lot of gray, I noticed. Do you think he uses Grecian Formula? Or that five-minute stuff? They could put that on him right before he goes on the air. If he sweated he might be in trouble, though."

"You didn't ask?"

"Don't be tacky."

We pulled into my driveway just as it began to mist. It was well above freezing so ice was no danger, but Woofer would miss his walk again. I told my burdened Southern Sister goodbye and went over to the igloo to check him out.

"Come inside a while," I told him.

He grudgingly agreed. He followed me into the house, I gave him a couple of dog biscuits, and he stretched out on his rug to nibble at them. Muffin eyed us from the center of the kitchen table. I took her down, gave her a couple of Pounce treats, and went to check my messages.

My only E-mail message was from someone advertising SEX SEX SEX on the Internet. I get quite a few of these ads, having wandered one day onto a Website called *Amazon Lovers* or something like that when I was trying to order a book. I think I am now on some kind of international list of large lesbians.

I deleted the SEX SEX SEX, which zipped me back to Haley's last message about the pope. I reread it and realized she was probably in Rome by then. I couldn't have been happier for her. This time last year she had been a widow, lonely, still grieving for what might have been with her husband, Tom, whose life had been severed by a drunk driver. Tom on his way home from work with flowers and a Valentine for Haley.

I touched the computer screen. "Be happy, darling."

There were three phone messages. One was a siding company, the second one wanted to sell us insurance, and the third one surprised me so I had to sit down.

"Patricia Anne?" It was a woman's voice and she was whispering, but I recognized her before she said, "This is Virginia. Please call me at 615-555-9678. I need some help. Bad."

In spite of the sinister sound of the message, I was so relieved to hear Virginia's voice, I said, "Yes!" Woofer and Muffin both jumped.

I looked at my watch. Mary Alice was at Debbie's, but maybe Richard and Luke had declared a truce and come back while we were eating with the Packards.

I dialed Sister's number. No Richard, or if

he was there he wasn't answering. I dialed Debbie's. One of the twins answered. Teeny (we're still trying to figure out why the twins call Mary Alice this) wasn't there, Aunt Pat, but did I want to speak to Brother? He was asleep, but she would wake him up.

"Fay?"

"May, Aunt Pat."

"I'd like to speak to your mama, darling."

"She's asleep. I'll wake her up."

"No, don't do that, May. Let her sleep."

"Okay. Bye." May hung up.

I played Virginia's message again and wrote the number down. After listening to it the second time, I realized that it was just as well that I hadn't been able to reach Luke. Virginia had specifically asked for me to call her.

Which I did. She answered "Hello" in a whisper.

"Virginia?" I whispered back.

"Patricia Anne? Oh, Patricia Anne."

"Where are you?"

"In a Holiday Inn Express in Nashville."

"Why are you in Nashville and why are we whispering?"

"I don't know." A normal voice. "My ass is in a sling, Patricia Anne."

"You mean with Luke? No way. He's going to be so relieved to hear you're okay that it's not going to matter what you've done. He's been worried to death, Virginia. Richard, too. He's here trying to find you."

"My baby's there?"

"We just got back from Chandler Mountain looking for you."

"Y'all stay away from Chandler Mountain, Patricia Anne. I saw what happened to Monk Crawford on CNN. God." Virginia's voice dropped to a whisper again. "I saw more than I should have."

I shivered. "You saw who killed him?"

"Of course not. But I saw my own car right there on CNN with Monk in it dead. Snakebit." Virginia began to cry. "He was a nice man, Patricia Anne."

"I'm sure he was."

"Good painter, too. The soffits never looked so good."

Enough.

"How did you want me to help you, Virginia?"

"I'm going to be charged with murder, Patricia Anne."

"You're not going to be charged with murder, Virginia."

"Why not?"

"Maybe because you didn't kill anybody?"

"But I did. He's lying right here on the floor."

I caught my breath. "Who are you talking about, Virginia?"

"Spencer Gordon. I killed him."

"Virginia," I said calmly. "Hang up and call 911."

"Told you my ass was in a sling."

The phone went dead. I looked frantically in my end table drawer for my address book. I can never remember Sister's car phone number. No book. I ran into the kitchen and looked in the junk drawer. No book. I thought maybe I should call Nashville 911. Could I do that? Could I call our 911 and have them transfer me? Oh, hell. I was rushing down the hall toward the bedroom when the phone rang. Please God, let it be Virginia. Let her say she was joking. Some sorry-ass joke, but I'd forgive her. Yes I would. Please God.

It was Sister.

"I just found out something about Eugene Mahall," she said.

"Virginia's in a Holiday Inn Express in Nashville with a man she just killed," I gasped. "She says he's lying on the floor and she killed him."

"What?"

"God's truth."

"A Holiday Inn Express? With all of those elegant hotels in Nashville?"

I hung up on her and realized immediately that I didn't know how to call her back. Not that it mattered. The woman didn't have walking-around sense. Nevertheless, I was relieved when the phone rang again.

I snatched it up. "Listen, Miss Snotty. I remember when you were happy with Bob's Tourist Court. Spent quite a few nights there, if my memory serves me correctly."

"Aunt Pat?"

"Oh, Debbie. Thank God."

"What's the matter?"

I went through Virginia's story again, and this time I got a sensible response.

"I'll call and talk to the manager of the motel, Aunt Pat. You keep trying to get Richard and Luke. I'm sure nothing bad has really happened." Then, "Wait a minute, Aunt Pat."

I waited.

"Sorry. I had to switch Brother to the other side. Now let me write this down. What's the man's name?"

"Spencer Gordon. I think he may be from Seattle."

"And it's a Holiday Inn Express."

"Nice places to stay. Fred and I stay in them all the time. AARP discounts."

"I'll call you back in a little while. And what was that about Bob's Tourist Court?"

"Ask your mother."

I sat on the edge of the bed and willed my blood pressure to go down. Relax, feet. Relax, hands. Relax, shoulders. I was on the beach at Destin and the sun was setting. A blue heron was wading into a tidal pool. It was not my fault that my sister didn't have biddy brains. It was not my fault that Virginia's ass was in a sling for killing a man in a Holiday Inn Express. I was calm and collected. My daughter was at this very moment having an audience with the pope. His blessings were flowing over me vicariously.

The phone rang and I jumped like I had been shot. Damn.

It was Fred. He had a hankering for corned beef and cabbage. Should he stop by Morrison's on the way home?

If he had a hankering for corned beef and cabbage, he'd better. And get some egg custard pie.

"Wait a minute," I said before he hung up. "I love you."

"I love you, too. Want to uncork some vintage Viagra tonight?"

Why not? I was feeling much better when I dialed Mary Alice's number again. And this time, Luke answered.

I asked to speak to Richard, but Luke immediately sensed something was wrong.

"Something about Virginia?"

"No, Luke. The President's trying to get in touch with him."

There was a sharp intake of breath, an excited mumbling, and Richard was on the phone in a second. "The President wants me? Did he say what for?"

He sounded so thrilled, I felt guilty bursting his bubble.

"It's your mama, Richard. I didn't want to tell your daddy on the phone. She's okay, but she's in a Holiday Inn Express in Nashville and says she's killed a man."

"The President called to tell me that? That was thoughtful, wasn't it?"

I hoped for a moment that this was an act he was putting on for his father, but the tone of his voice was too excited.

"Very thoughtful," I agreed. "He also suggested that you might want to see about her. Debbie's calling the manager at the motel to find out what's going on. But I think you ought to take over from here."

"Right. Thank you, Cousin Pat."

"You're welcome, Richard. Be sure and let the President know how things turn out."

I hung up and looked down at Woofer who was drooling over his Milkbone. "Want to run for Congress?"

I slipped on some jeans, a sweatshirt, and my Bullwinkle fuzzy slippers while I waited on Debbie's call. I was worried about Virginia, but the talk with Richard had lightened my spirits. I turned on the gas logs in the den fireplace and fixed myself a cup of hot chocolate. Muffin jumped up beside me on the sofa, and Woofer stretched out in front of the fire.

This, I was thinking, was what January afternoons should all be like. I even managed to finish the hot chocolate and was dozing when the phone rang.

"The man's not dead," Mary Alice announced. "They're taking him to Vanderbilt Hospital, but they think he just had a spell of some kind."

"What kind of spell? Virginia said he was lying on the floor and he was obviously unconscious if she thought he was dead."

"How should I know, Mouse? Maybe one like Aunt Gracie used to have. Remember how she would fall out? Get that look in her eye and we'd know to catch her. Good thing she was little."

"Have you talked to Richard? I told him his mother was in Nashville and okay except for maybe having killed a man."

"He's trying to get a flight out now, but he may end up driving if he can't get out soon. He's all excited about the President calling him."

"Our family is blessed."

"We are. Imagine the President taking such a personal interest in Richard."

"Imagine."

"I'll call you if I hear anything else. Henry's fixed pot roast for supper."

"Enjoy."

I was in a good humor when Fred came in. So good, in fact, that we uncorked the Viagra before we ate the corned beef and cabbage. Totally missed *Wheel of Fortune*.

"A spell?" He asked as we were eating our egg custard pie. "Virginia called you to say the guy was dead and he had had some kind of a spell?"

"All I know is what Sister said. They took him to Vanderbilt Hospital."

"Does this have something to do with the snake-handling preacher?"

"I doubt it. I don't know what's going on. Sister thinks Monk Crawford took Virginia to Nashville to meet this man. I guess it's possible."

"Mary Alice say any more about Virgil? I thinks she's got her a good one this time. He was telling me the best places at Smith Lake to catch bass. He's got a cabin up there."

"Well, let him break the news to her."

"True."

I'm sure both of us had the same mental picture of Sister in a lake cabin cleaning bass.

We were in bed asleep by nine o'clock. Sometime later the phone rang and woke me up.

"Migraine," Sister said.

"What?"

"The Gordon guy is going to be okay. He had a migraine attack, took some new medicine he had, and was sleeping it off."

"On the floor? He must have taken a hell of a dose."

"Well, Virginia said she didn't have her glasses on and must have guessed wrong when she gave it to him. Do you suppose Aunt Gracie had migraines? Remember how funny her eyes looked?"

"I think Aunt Gracie took paregoric, Sister. I'm going back to sleep now."

"Well, I never did tell you what I found about Eugene Mahall."

"What about him?"

"He can walk as good as you and I can."

This woke me up.

"Who says?"

"I was talking to Virgil on the car phone telling him where we'd been and he told me. Said he'd seen him himself. Said he went out to his house to question him about Louellen's disappearance. You know, the country singer he married who kept jumping into the legustrum trying to commit suicide? And you know those glass panels on either side of the door? Virgil saw him walking down the hall big as life. But when he opened the door, he was in the wheelchair."

"Insurance fraud?"

"That's what I said. But Virgil says probably not, that when he collected the insurance he really was crippled up."

"What would be the purpose then?"

"I have no idea, Mouse. Why do you always think I know all the answers?"

"I'm going to sleep now."

I hung up, but I didn't go back to sleep for

a long time. Why would Eugene Mahall want everyone to think he couldn't walk?

"I'm scared," I heard Betsy say.

What a can of worms. Basket of snakes.

I finally got up and fixed some decaffeinated tea. Ended up sleeping on the sofa with Muffin.

Chapter Sixteen

The next morning, I was sitting at the kitchen table reading the paper and having a second cup of coffee when there was a knock on my back door.

"Any sweetrolls and coffee?" Officer Bo Mitchell of the Birmingham Police Department asked when I opened the door.

"For you, always."

I hugged Bo and took her coat.

"Lord, you're skinny, girl!"

Bo twirled to show off her new figure. "One twenty-five. And that's it. I'm at the sticking point now. So one sweetroll and that's it."

"You look wonderful." And she did. Bo has the most beautiful skin, a light milk chocolate color and her eyes have a slightly Asian cast. She is also one of the nicest people I know, funny and brave. Her friendship is one of the best things that has happened to me since I retired from teaching.

"Sit down and I'll get you some coffee."

I put her coat over a chair in the den while she sat down at the table.

"Where's Joanie this morning?" I asked. Joanie Salk is Bo's partner.

"We had the night shift. I just came to hear about your trip. How's Haley doing?"

"So good you wouldn't believe." I put a cup of coffee in front of Bo and got some sweetrolls from the refrigerator and stuck them in the microwave. "She's loving being married and living in Warsaw. And, Bo, guess what? She and Philip are in Rome today. They've got an audience with the pope. Not one of those big things with a crowd, but a small group. They're really going to get blessed by him personally."

Bo has a terrific grin. Every time I see it I think of the thousands of dollars we spent on our kids' teeth just praying for smiles like that and missing it by a mile. "I'm so happy for her. That's great."

"Yes, it is."

She reached for the sweetener. "How's Mary Alice? She and Fred get along on the Concorde?"

"They did fine. Peter Jennings was on the plane with us coming back so she rearranged everyone's seats."

"She get engaged to him?"

The microwave dinged and I took the rolls out.

"He slept. I can't believe she didn't wake him up."

"The poor soul. He doesn't know what he missed."

I put the rolls between us and sat down.

"She's fallen in love since we got home, though."

"Who with?" Bo took a sweetroll and blew on it to cool it.

"A man named Virgil Stuckey. The sheriff of St. Clair County."

"Really? I know Sheriff Stuckey. He's a nice guy."

Bo looked up suddenly. "The sheriff of St. Clair County? Y'all been messing around up there, getting in trouble?"

"Well, you heard about the snake-handling murders?"

Bo shook her head in disbelief. "Damn. Should have known."

"Well, it's Pukey Lukey's wife's fault. She ran off with the snake handler. At least, Luke thought she had."

Bo nodded and took a big bite of her sweet-roll. By the time I finished telling her all that had happened, she had eaten two rolls and had finished her second cup of coffee. The telling, eating, and drinking were punctuated with Bo's favorite expression, "Do, Jesus!" Bo is a wonderful listener, probably one of the reasons she's such a good policeman.

"Sounds like a mess," she said when she realized I had finished the story with the man in Vanderbilt Hospital who had the migraine attack and Virginia having thought he was dead.

"It is," I agreed. "Thank goodness Virginia's shown up. We're out of it now. It's up to the sheriff."

"That'll be the day." Bo licked some icing from her finger. "You and Mary Alice are going to help him out by finding out who did it, aren't you?"

"Nope, Miss Smart Aleck. But I am going to tell him he needs to take a good look at a man named Joe Baker. We met him yesterday and you could just see the mean in his eyes. You know how that is?"

Bo nodded that she recognized mean in peoples' eyes.

"He's Monk Crawford's brother-in-law, and now that Susan and Monk are both dead, he'll probably be the chief snake handler."

"Now that's something to aspire to, isn't it? Snakes. Yuck. You know," Bo stuck her finger in the crumbs on her plate and licked them off, "my mama was the dickens on potty training. Had us all out of diapers by the time we were eighteen months old. But last fall I was spreading pine straw under my shrubbery and picked up a handful with a little snake in it. Lord! I peed my pants."

I laughed. "What kind of snake was it?"

"Don't know. I threw him a winding and went to take a shower and wash my clothes." Bo placed both of her hands on the table and spread her fingers out in what looked liked a gesture of surrender. "Deliver me from those things."

We sat quietly for a moment and I remembered that I hadn't told her the most important thing of all.

"Debbie had her baby, Bo. They're fine."

Bo's smile beamed again. "That's wonderful. Mary Alice beside herself?"

"Just about it. She'd given up on grandchildren until Debbie got pregnant with the twins, you know."

"Haley will be next."

"I hope so." I pointed toward Bo's cup. She shook her head no and said she needed to get on home and get some sleep.

"Well, let me ask you something before you go. Susan Crawford's body in the church? The way it was laid out? I've been thinking about it. Have you ever run up on any bodies that are fixed just so, with their clothes fixed neatly, and even their hair looking like it had been brushed?"

"I get the drive-by shootings and the ODs under the interstate. They're laid out all right, just the way they quit breathing."

"Well, what about women murderers? Do you think they would tend to straighten up the bodies more?"

"Patricia Anne, have you lost your mind? Of course not. They'd get the hell out as quick as any man. Quicker, maybe. You think tidying up is some kind of innate female thing, regardless of the circumstances? Lord, girl!

"Tell you what, though." Bo followed me into the den where I had put her coat. "We did have a case in West End where an eighty-year-old man killed his wife who had Alzheimer's. Smothered her with a pillow. He had her all bathed and in her prettiest nightgown when he called us. Even had makeup on her."

Bo held out her arms for her coat. "Only time I ever cried at a murder scene. And didn't feel a damn bit bad about it. A man named Jeff Maloney answered the call with me and he was sniffling, too. Damn."

"And someone broke Susan Crawford's neck and then laid her out like they loved her."

Bo slipped into her coat. "Maybe it wasn't the same person. Maybe someone found her dead and took her into the church."

I hadn't thought of that possibility. But after Bo left with promises of calling soon, I had Joe Baker killing Susan and Monk finding the body and laying her out in the church. Or Eugene Mahall killing Susan (I could think of no reason for my suspicion except that he had lied about walking), and Betsy finding the body. She could have been the woman Luke swore he saw in the church. But that didn't make sense. Betsy would have called the police immediately if she had found Susan's body. Surely she would have.

I finished loading the dishwasher and turned it on. One thing I was sure of now. Whoever had put Susan Crawford's body in the church, whoever had straightened her clothes and combed her hair, had cared deeply for her.

It was a beautiful sunny day. The temperature was supposed to be in the sixties with rain that night and much colder weather the next day. Muffin was lying in the bay window watching two squirrels trying to get sunflower seeds from my squirrelproof bird feeder that really works. The squirrels jump on the wooden perch and their weight closes the feeder. A remarkable invention except I feel so sorry for the squirrels after they've worked a long time, that I'll go and throw some seeds on the ground for them.

Woofer and I took a quick walk. Most of the Christmas decorations were down by now, but there were a couple of holdouts. There's a house a block away from us that has a chimney on the front. They put their wreath up Thanksgiving and take it down Easter. Don't ask. But it's a good way to give directions in February and March. "Go past the wreath house, turn left…"

I had thought I would have a message from Mary Alice, that she might have heard from Richard, but there was nothing but a dial tone. I turned on the computer; not even the SEX SEX SEX people were trying to communicate with me this morning.

I got in the shower feeling slightly depressed and knowing why. The last couple of months had been so busy, planning for the trip to Warsaw, the trip itself, Christmas, Brother's birth, Virginia's disappearance, and the whole Chandler Mountain snake-handling affair. A morning by myself was a letdown. Next week, I would start tutoring again at the middle school. Next week, I would shampoo the rugs and maybe invite some people for dinner. Arthur and Mitzi from next door, Frances Zata, of course, if she was in town and not in

Destin. I let the hot water run over my head and relaxed. Soon, mixed with the smell of shampoo was the smell of bacon frying. It was a pleasant smell, one the aromatherapy people should consider using. A smell that shouldn't have been in my house, but that didn't alarm me because I figured I knew the source.

I rinsed my hair, put on my white terry-cloth robe, and headed for the kitchen.

"Why don't you get some real bacon," Sister complained. "All I could find was this turkey stuff."

"Lower in cholesterol."

She was sitting at my table with what appeared to be several pieces of French toast and half a pound of bacon on the plate in front of her.

"Did you fix me some?" I asked.

"You can have some of this. I think my eyes were bigger than my stomach."

I would not answer that.

I got a plate and helped myself to a piece of French toast and a couple of pieces of bacon. Sister pushed the bottle of syrup toward me.

"Unusual hairdo." I couldn't resist. Sister's hair was pulled back into random patches, some of them caught with bobby pins.

"I've been to Delta Hairlines. It's the Dharma look."

I'm sure I looked blank.

"You know, Dharma from *Dharma and Greg,* the television show. Don't you and Fred ever watch anything but *Wheel of Fortune* and *Biography?*"

209

"We're always in a hurry to get to bed."

"You wish."

I poured syrup over the French toast. "You hear from Richard and Luke this morning?"

"Richard called while I was eating breakfast."

I pointed to the French toast. "What's this, then?"

Sister didn't miss a beat. "Brunch. Anyway, he ended up driving because there wasn't a direct flight until this morning and he said it was quicker than having to fly through Atlanta and change planes."

"How's his mama?"

"Feisty enough to tell Luke she was filing for divorce."

"Must have regained her feist when she found out she wasn't a felon."

Sister frowned at me and chomped into a piece of bacon.

"What about the Gordon guy? Is he going to be okay?"

Sister nodded, chewing. When she swallowed she said, "They met on the Internet. I don't know any of the details. I guess we'll find out this afternoon, though. They're coming back to my house. Virgil's going to meet them there at three o'clock to grill her."

"Gonna grill her, huh?"

Sister speared another piece of French toast and held it in the air. A drop of syrup dripped onto her plate.

"Should be interesting. You want to come?"

You bet I did. I wanted to know what had happened on Chandler Mountain, things that Virginia might have the answers for.

Things that the Chandler Mountain booger couldn't be blamed for, things that Betsy Mahall was frightened of.

On a hell-warmed-over scale of one to ten, Virginia's looks would warrant a solid eight. Granted, the afternoon light in Sister's sunroom was not flattering to anyone older than Tiffany, who was placing snacks on the coffee table and smiling at Richard (obviously this was going to be an informal interrogation), but Virginia looked rough. Her hair was a mahogany red, pulled straight back and either greased down with VO5 or in bad need of a shampoo. There were dark circles under her eyes and her lips looked strange, puffy. Surely Luke hadn't hit her.

I caught Sister's eye, nodded slightly toward Virginia, and touched my lips.

She mouthed something I didn't understand.

"What?" I mouthed back.

She reached into the end-table drawer, and in a moment handed me a Post-it with "Collagen" written on it. I folded the paper and put it in my pocket.

Virginia picked up her coffee cup and I watched with interest to see if she dribbled. She didn't. I think I was equating collagen with novocaine.

The six of us were sitting in a circle. Virgil hadn't minded at all when I showed up. In fact, he had said that maybe Mary Alice and I could remind him of some things that he might forget.

So far, between snacking and wondering if the repairs on the interstate to Nashville would ever be finished, this could be an ordinary tea party. Even Bubba Cat got down from his heating pad on the kitchen counter and came to lie in the sun right at Luke's feet. A dangerous place, considering that Luke was a strange green color.

Virgil finally put his coffee cup down, though, got out his notebook, and got down to business.

Yes, Virginia said, she had met Spencer Gordon on the Internet, had frequently gone into a chat room with him. Luke got up, stepped over Bubba and disappeared down the hall. We heard the bathroom door slam.

Virginia ignored the interruption. Spencer was a nice man. They had ballroom dancing in common.

"I didn't know you danced, Mama," Richard said.

Virginia pursed her new lips and looked at her son. "Your father doesn't. I do. When I tango, Richard, I can lift my leg over my partner's shoulder."

The congressman looked startled.

Virginia turned to us. "That impressed Spencer. His wife doesn't tango. Or do much else, apparently."

Virgil wrote something in his notebook, just one word, probably "tango," and told Virginia to go ahead with her story which turned out to be fairly logical.

There was going to be a Seniors' Swing Convention in Nashville. Spencer had invited her to meet him there and she had agreed since it was just a hop, skip, and a jump from Columbus, you know.

Virginia reached over, got an olive from the coffee table, and chewed it thoughtfully while we waited. We heard the toilet flush down the hall.

"But then," Virginia said, wiping her fingers on a napkin, "I got to thinking what did I know about this man? He could be an ax murderer for all I knew. And I was about to back out when Holden Crawford showed up to paint the house."

"What did he have to do with it?" Richard wanted to know.

"I invited him in for lunch one day and just happened to tell him about the convention and how I'd love to go. And he said, 'I'll take you and check the guy out for you. You can tell him I'm your brother.' So that's what we did."

"You did what, Mama?" Richard's voice was so loud that Bubba got up and stalked back into the kitchen. "You didn't know him any more than you did the guy in Nashville."

"Of course I did, Richard. He was a nice man."

"He was a snake handler, Mama."

"Well, yes he was, Son. But he was still a nice man, and I didn't know about the snakes until I saw it on CNN. That's what started Spencer's problems, too. He was taken aback by the fact that my brother was a snake handler who had been murdered. He said he was seeing zippers across his eyes. I should have known something was wrong."

"Will Alec had migraines," Sister said. "His always started with zigzag lights, too. Like zippers. I'm surprised that Gordon guy didn't have some of that new medicine to stop them."

"He should have." Virginia reached for another olive. The floor above us creaked. Luke had gone upstairs.

Virgil looked as if he were taken aback and seeing zippers, too, but he took a deep breath and asked Virginia to tell him about the couple of days she had spent on Chandler Mountain.

"Boring. Holden didn't even have cable. But he said he had some business he had to take care of before we went to Nashville. And, no, sheriff, I don't have any idea what it was. A couple of guys came by. One was his brother-in-law." Virginia frowned. "Holden didn't like him. They were having a fuss about something. And his daughter-in-law, Susan, came by with the grandchildren. Cute as they could be. Susan was, too." Virginia sighed. "I can't believe she's dead, too. Holden really loved her and those children."

"You said a couple of guys?" Virgil asked.

"A young man Holden said had a crush on Susan. He just came to the door and they talked a minute."

"Did he have a beard?" I asked. I was thinking of Albert Lee Packard. To Virginia he would be a young man.

"I don't remember one."

Then it wasn't Albert Lee with his memorable Spanish moss.

"What kind of car was this man driving?" Virgil wanted to know.

"I didn't see it."

Richard stood up. "I think I'd better go see about Daddy. He nearly got himself killed, you know, Mama, looking for you."

"Should have learned to dance."

Richard stomped out, and Virgil closed his notebook which, best as I could tell, had maybe a dozen words written in it.

"Mrs. Nelson, I think we'd better continue this tomorrow in my office. Okay?"

"I'll bring her," Sister volunteered immediately. "What time?"

"I'll take her," I said. "I've got to take Betsy Mahall's key back to her anyway."

"We'll all go," Sister said.

Virgil ran the palm of his hand across his mouth, a gesture that I would learn to recognize meant, "I give up."

"About two," he said. He reached in his pocket and pulled out Susan Crawford's cameo. "And, Patricia Anne, if you're going to see Betsy, give her this. We've checked it out."

"I'd be happy to. It'll make her feel better."

"Oh, I reconize that," Virginia said. "Holden's daughter-in-law was wearing that when we went to the grocery in Oneonta and I think one of the babies must have broken the chain. I found it in the car on the way to Tennessee. Holden was supposed to give it back to her."

But neither of them had lived to see the other again.

"It belongs to her daughter now." I slipped the cameo into my purse.

215

Chapter Seventeen

The next morning was what Mama always called a thin morning. The sun wasn't quite breaking through, but you could see its shape behind the clouds. A dry cold front had come through during the night, and the temperature had dropped at least twenty degrees.

I called Betsy Mahall, told her that Virginia had shown up in Nashville at a Seniors' Swing Convention, but that Virgil Stuckey wanted to question her about the couple of days she had been on Chandler Mountain. Would it be all right if I returned the key this afternoon? I didn't mention the cameo; I had decided that I would wait and surprise her with that.

"About what time, Mrs. Hollowell?" She sounded listless, tired.

"A little after two?" I hesitated and then added, "I've got a surprise for you."

There was a pause on the other end of the line. Maybe I should just tell her I had the cameo.

Then, "Mrs. Hollowell, do you think we could meet up at Monk's house? I had planned to go up there this afternoon and start looking around, seeing what should be saved for Jamie and Ethan and what should be sold." She sighed. "I guess I'll have to do the same thing at Susan's, but I'm going to have to wait a while on that."

"Did you go to Monk's funeral?" I asked.

"No. Terry did. I had to keep the children. He said it was very subdued, actually."

Betsy sounded as if she were about to cry.

"Are the children okay?" I asked.

"Fine. I guess I'll bring them this afternoon. Monk's house is babyproofed. They stayed there with him a lot."

I wondered if babyproofing meant keeping the snakes under the bed in a box, but I just said I would see her a little after two and hung up.

I called Mary Alice and told her that I was going up to Chandler Mountain so I'd go in my car.

"Go with me and Virginia," she said. "I'll take you up there."

"No, I'll go in my car. That way I won't be in a hurry."

"Wait a minute," Sister said. I heard her put the phone down and close the door.

"You don't understand," she said when she came back. "I think the collagen's seeped up into Virginia's brain or the mahagony dye has seeped down. Or both. The woman's certifiable, Mouse."

"What's she done?"

"Right now she's teaching Tiffany how to tango."

I giggled.

"Not funny. You got any of that Ritalin stuff left from when you taught school? I think she needs some."

"You think they gave it to the teachers to hand out like candy?"

"From what I read in the papers."

"No, I don't have any Ritalin. But it does sound like she might have some problems. Get Richard to take her to a doctor."

"He and Luke won't come downstairs. They hear the tango music." Sister paused. "The whole damn neighborhood hears the music."

"Then I know I'm going in my car. 'Bye, Sister."

"Wait a minute."

"What?"

I could practically hear the wheels in her brain turning.

"I swear I'll forgive you for losing my Shirley Temple doll."

I knew she was lying. We'll go to our graves with her holding that against me. "Fifty-six curls, Patricia Anne," she's been saying for fifty-five years. "Fifty-six perfect little corkscrew curls, and those precious little red leather shoes with one button, and you lost her."

The fact that she had even mentioned the subject of forgiving me for Shirley Temple, a crime I didn't even remember committing, told me how desperate she was, though.

"Make Richard take her," I said.

"But Virgil is expecting me."

"Virgil has a pot belly. You can't say anything about Fred's anymore."

Silence. Then, "I know, but it's okay."

Of course I ended up going with them. Maybe I just lost my mind and thought there was a slight chance that Sister really might forgive me for the Shirley Temple doll. Maybe I was still under the influence of jet lag. Or maybe, God forbid, I'd never figured out how to keep Sister from bossing me around. I think I know which "maybe" it was.

So we headed back up I-59, three old ladies on a thin day in January in a Jaguar. I was getting familiar with the territory. On a billboard just past Trussville was an advertisement for Schaeffer Eye Center, a pair of glasses with lights running around the frames. It reminded me of the billboard in *The Great Gatsby*, the all-seeing eye.

Virginia kept reaching over to change the radio station to dance music. It would instantly revert to WBHM and classical music.

"Something's wrong with this radio," Virginia said.

"Got good taste," Mary Alice said, her hand hiding the controls on the steering wheel.

"Huh." Virginia gave up on the radio, pulled off her shoes, and propped her feet on the dashboard. Her fingers played a piano tune on the knees of her black slacks. I tried to figure out the tune and finally decided it was either "Jingle Bells" or "Chopsticks."

"Have you heard from the Gordon guy?" I asked.

Virginia didn't miss a note. "Gone home to Seattle. He's fine."

The tune changed. Virginia's thumbs slid across the tops of her knees. A tango?

"I don't think he was competition material anyway. Too double-jointed."

"Shame," Mary Alice said.

Virginia looked at her suspiciously, decided that Sister really was commiserating with her and agreed that yes, it was a shame. Especially in the jitterbug. You couldn't have those knees suddenly popping out at a funny angle.

"How old was this man?" Mary Alice asked.

"Late sixties, I guess. Maybe seventy."

"Sure you weren't mistaking a wobble for a double-joint?"

"Huh. Think I don't know a wobble from a double-joint?" Virginia resumed her piano playing. By the time we got to Ashville where the sheriff's substation was, I think she was playing "Flight of the Bumblebee."

"I'm nervous," she admitted as Mary Alice pulled into a parking place marked VIS-ITOR.

"Nothing to be nervous about." I said. "Sheriff Stuckey's a nice man, and I'll be back to get y'all in about an hour."

I got the reaction I was expecting. Sister hit the curb.

"Hell, Mary Alice," Virginia grumbled. "Why don't you just run into the building?" She had been leaning over putting on her shoes and had smacked her head against the dashboard. She pulled the visor down and examined her forehead in the mirror. "I may have a bruise."

"No, you won't. And we'll be back in about an hour. More like an hour and a half since we've got to go up that mountain."

"You're not coming in? I thought you were coming in with me."

"Patricia Anne knocks down mailboxes."

"She does?" Virginia looked back at me. "Why?"

"I hit one mailbox when I was fifteen and learning to drive," I said.

"Pure luck. She aims for them all. And she keeps thinking she's going to trick me into letting her drive my Jag."

"Well, my goodness." Virginia collected her purse and opened the door. "Won't you at least come in for a minute?"

"I'll come speak to Virgil a minute. Invite him to supper." Sister carefully removed the keys and told me I could get in the front seat.

"Luke's a terrible driver, too," I heard Virginia telling Sister as they walked away. "Maybe it's genetic."

When we got to Monk Crawford's house there was no sign of Betsy's car.

"You've got the key. We could go in," Sister suggested, pulling into the graveled area between the house and church.

"I don't think we should do that."

"Why not? We were in there going through everything the other day."

Fortunately I didn't have to answer. Betsy Mahall walked out onto the porch and waved at us. "Y'all come on in.

"Terry brought me," she explained as we

joined her. "He had to go to Oneonta on business. He'll be back after a while."

"Where are the children?" I asked as we went into the house.

"They're up at Miss Beulah's. Y'all want some coffee? I've got some made."

"Aren't you scared some books will fall on them?" Sister asked.

Betsy smiled. "You've seen Albert Lee's loot."

"His treasure." I reached in my coat pocket and handed Betsy the house key. "Here, before I forget it. And thank you."

She slipped it into her pants pocket. "You're welcome. Is your cousin all right?"

"Luke or Virginia?" Sister asked.

"Both."

"They're okay. Virgil Stuckey's talking to Virginia right this minute. Not that I think he'll get anything out of her."

"Well, y'all pull off your coats and sit down. I'm not doing a thing in the world but running around in circles here."

She went into the kitchen while we pulled off our coats and sat down. The space heater in the fireplace had been lighted long enough to make the room cozy.

"I'm tempted to just call the Salvation Army and tell them to come clean the house out," Betsy called. "But then I get to thinking that what's here belonged to Jamie and Ethan's grandparents and I know I ought to keep some of it. Things like their grandmother's cedar chest, and Monk's tools. Ethan might love to have them when he grows up."

She came back into the living room with a tray with three cups of coffee on it, sugar, and cream. She placed the tray on the table in front of us, pulled one of the chairs over, and sat down.

"I'm so tired," she admitted, reaching for one of the cups.

"Do you have help at your house?"

Trust Sister not to beat around the bush.

"No. I told my father-in-law last night that we may have to at least get a maid service to come in once a week. He's strange, though, about people coming into the house. Almost paranoid." Betsy sipped her coffee. "I guess because he's disabled. He won't even get anybody to help him, you know, like bathing and stuff. Terry has to do it."

Sister and I glanced at each other while Betsy continued. Why would a person who could walk do this to his family?

"And I know he could drive a car. They make them for all kinds of handicapped people. But he won't even try. Terry takes him to the bank every day. And wherever else he wants to go."

"Well, how did you manage when you were working?" I asked.

"I just walked out the door, closed it, and was gone for eight hours." Betsy put her cup down. Her hand was shaking, I noticed. "I can't do that with Jamie and Ethan to take care of."

Suddenly she smiled. "But you wouldn't believe how thrilled Terry is to have them there. The children. He doesn't even want to leave them to go to work."

"What about your father-in-law?" I asked. "Is it all right with him?"

"He's worse than Terry. Rides them around on his wheelchair." Betsy shrugged. "So we'll be all right. I've just got to adjust to being a mother and count my blessings."

"Speaking of which." I reached in my purse and pulled out the Ziploc bag with the cameo in it. "I think you'll be happy this showed up."

Betsy held out her hand and took the bag. Her eyes widened.

"The cameo," she whispered.

She undid the bag, took the cameo out, and held it to her cheek in a touching gesture.

"Oh, thank you, Mrs. Hollowell. Thank you so much."

"You're welcome, Betsy. I'm just so glad it was found."

"Where was it? The church?" She held the cameo out and looked at it. "I looked over every inch of the church."

"It was in Virginia's car," I said reluctantly.

"The car they found Monk's body in?" Her hands closed around the cameo, clutched it.

"Between the seats."

The "Oh" from Betsy was more a breath than a word. The blood drained from her face; she jumped up and rushed down the hall to the bathroom.

Mary Alice turned around to me. "She's upset," she explained as if I had totally missed the obvious.

"Well, of course she is, Sister. She didn't let me finish. She probably thinks that the cameo being in Monk's car means that the same person killed Susan and Monk both. One of the snake handlers like that Joe Baker."

"It's still possible. The murderer could have found the cameo, put it in his pocket, and dropped it when he put the basket of snakes in Virginia's car."

"That's pretty far-fetched."

"But not impossible. Think about it."

"I don't want to think about it. Just thinking about snakes gives me the creeps."

Sister got up and went to stand by the fireplace, holding out her hands to the space heater. She glanced at her watch. "We need to go."

I nodded at the hall. "Well, we can't leave until we know she's all right."

A ray of sun spliced across the white vinyl floor; the clouds were breaking up.

"The Packard guy," Mary Alice said when we heard the sound of tires on the gravel driveway. "Lord, he needs to shave." She went to open the door.

"Hey, Mrs. Crane. I saw your car," I heard him say. "Did you find your cousin?"

"She was in Nashville at a dancing convention."

I heard Albert chuckle. "I figured she was all right. I told you Monk was running an underground railroad for frustrated women."

"Come on in."

"No, thanks. I've got to get home. I promised Mama I'd help her figure out how to stay out of jail. That woman. I swear. When somebody pays her two hundred dollars cash for a quilt, she doesn't think she should pay tax on it. The IRS is disagreeing."

"Well, you tell your mama she has my sympathy. I don't think she should have to, either."

"I'll do that. Has Betsy left?"

Sister shook her head. "She's still here. You want to come in?"

"No. Just tell her I'll see her later. And I'm glad your cousin showed up."

"Thanks. We are, too. Tell your mama hey." Sister closed the door and turned to me. "Imagine charging that poor old lady tax on quilts."

No way I was going to get drawn into this.

"Was that Albert?" Betsy was standing in the hall doorway, wiping her face with a washcloth.

Sister nodded. "He said he'd talk to you later."

"How are you feeling?" I asked. I already knew the answer. She looked like hell.

"Better. I'm sorry." Betsy came over and sat back in the chair she had vacated so quickly. She held the washcloth against her throat. "I don't know. Things just hit me all of a sudden."

"I can understand that," I said.

She held up the cameo. "But I thank you so much for this, Mrs. Hollowell."

"I'm glad Jamie will have it. And, Betsy, my cousin Virginia found it in her car when they were on their way to Tennessee. Susan and the children went grocery shopping with her and she says she thinks one of the children might have broken the chain."

Betsy nodded. "Thank you."

I started collecting the coffee cups, but Betsy stopped me. "I'll get those."

"Don't be silly. You just sit there and get to feeling better."

"No, really. I'm fine."

Mary Alice looked at her watch. I stood up.

"Well, if you ever need me for anything, you just call," I told Betsy.

"I will. Thanks."

She got up and walked to the door with us. I still wasn't sure we ought to leave, but Mary Alice was halfway to the car by the time I gave Betsy a hug.

"Virgil's coming to dinner," she said when I got in the Jaguar. "I've got to go by By Request and pick something up. I guess I'll have to feed the whole Nelson clan again, too. Unless you want to invite them."

"Send them to Morrison's Cafeteria."

Gravel spun under the tires as Sister backed out and headed up the mountain.

"What's that rattle?" I asked. "Did you shake something loose when you hit the curb at the sheriff's?"

"Of course not. If I'd hit the curb that hard the air bags would have deployed."

"Well, something's loose." The noise seemed to be coming from the back. I turned and shrieked just as the biggest rattlesnake I had ever seen in my life struck where my arm had been and where Sister's hand was now.

Sister centered the Packards' mailbox and the airbags deployed. It was a nightmare that I would live over and over again for months, being engulfed in an airbag with my last view being that of a huge poisonous snake latched on to my sister's hand.

Chapter Eighteen

"So y'all are handlers. You told me the other day you didn't handle snakes."

We were traveling down the mountain to Oneonta in the same ambulance that Luke had traveled in to the hospital. The same two young women had picked up all two hundred fifty pounds of Sister and slid her easily into the back of the ambulance. The same driver. The same paramedic, Tammy, sitting across from me.

Sister was strapped on the gurney, the hand the snake had bitten encased in what looked like Styrofoam. Her eyes were closed and she was deathly pale, but every few minutes she managed to say, "This is all your fault, Patricia Anne."

And, believe it or not, I'd say, "I know. I'm sorry."

Had I suggested that Sister accompany me to Chandler Mountain? Ever? Had I put the snake in the car? The only thing I was guilty of was moving my arm just as the snake struck, allowing it to hit Sister's hand. Nevertheless, I felt guilty as hell and kept agreeing that it was, indeed, my fault.

"We're not handlers," I assured Tammy. "We're just having a streak of bad luck."

"God's truth," from the gurney.

"God's truth," Tammy agreed. "You feeling okay?" She was asking me.

Actually I felt like I'd been in a boxing match with Mohammed Ali. No, Cassius Clay before he was Mohammed Ali. When he was still slinging those twenty-year-old punches in every direction and winning the Olympics. Air bags save lives; I'm all for them. But my tiny body is no match for them. It hurt to take a deep breath, and my face felt like the top layer of skin was gone.

"You may have to help me out of the ambulance," I said. "I'm getting stiffer by the minute."

"This is all your fault, Patricia Anne," came from the gurney.

"Are you hurting bad?" I asked Sister.

"Of course I'm hurting. And I'm feeling dizzy and nauseated, and I've wrecked my car."

"She's going to be fine," Tammy assured me. "We got to her in plenty of time." Then to Sister, "You haven't been drinking strychnine, have you?"

Sister opened one eye and looked at Tammy. "Of course not. Why would I drink strychnine?"

"Oh, that's right. You're not a handler. Some of them drink it."

"Strychnine? Like the poison?"

"Sometimes."

Mary Alice groaned.

"How's your log cabin coming along?" I asked Tammy.

"Haven't done much on it the last couple of days." Tammy tapped at a gauge, picked up a telephone, and read some numbers into it. She turned back to me. "Been too busy."

"Lots of emergencies?"

She nodded. "People wait until after Christmas to die. Happens that way every year. Never fails."

"That makes sense," Sister said. "You don't want to miss Christmas. I bought these purple boots in Warsaw, Poland, this Christmas."

Tammy lifted the blanket and looked at the boots. "I forgot about those. We need to get them off. We don't want anything constricting your extremities."

"My extremities aren't constricted. Don't you dare touch my boots." Sister tried to sit up, but the straps allowed only a sideways movement of her head.

"She's fond of the boots," I explained.

Tammy shrugged and brushed her bangs out of her eyes. They immediately fell back in. I'll bet her mother was dying to get to her with the scissors. Or some bobby pins. I glanced at Sister. The Dharma look was a good one if you were going to be bitten by a snake and hit a mailbox. You couldn't tell if it was messed up or not.

"How did y'all get tangled up with that snake anyway?" Tammy asked, giving up on the boots. "The guy who called us said it was a huge one."

"Somebody put it in our car." I shivered

and looked out at the now familiar lime-stone-rock walls of the road, at the leaning pines. They looked, I realized, like the universal sign for PICNIC AREA, a sign that has always bothered me because the tree looks like it may fall at any minute on the unwary picnickers. The trees along this road loomed the same way.

Tammy tapped the gauges again. Either they were defective or she didn't believe what she was seeing. "Why would they do that?"

"Crazy," Sister muttered.

I touched the right side of my rib cage. Definitely painful. I tried to take a deep breath. Definitely painful. I would need to be checked out at the hospital, too.

I suddenly felt very sleepy. I rested my head against Sister's gurney. And when I closed my eyes, I saw the rattler striking Sister's hand. A hand that had been encased in a leather driving glove.

My eyes popped open.

"Tell the children I love them, Mouse." Sister whispered faintly.

"Tell them yourself."

I turned to Tammy. "Is she really bitten?"

"Oh, yes, ma'am. Not as bad as she would have been without those gloves, but the fangs went through a little bit."

"So she's just a little bit bit."

Tammy looked thoughtful. "Well, a little bit bit is something you have to see about when the snake's that big. She may need some antivenom. If she was small she definitely would."

Sister opened her eyes, frowned at Tammy, and closed them again.

"You got no idea who put the snake in your car?" Tammy asked. "Must have been a handler. You can't find big rattlers in the woods in January."

"Some fool," Sister said.

I was concentrating on not breathing too deeply. I put my head against the gurney again and thought about what had happened. Obviously the snake had been a warning. The person who put it in the car knew that even if we were bitten badly, we were close to help. There was a phone in the car and paramedics nearby. Of course, we could have gone over the side of the mountain and been killed. Obviously, the person hadn't cared.

Fortunately, we had hit the mailbox and Albert Lee Packard had come rushing out.

Sister had hit a mailbox with her Jaguar. I felt a giggle burbling up. It was immediately stifled by pain. Damn.

"Snake!" Sister had screeched, batting against the airbag, yanking the door open, and nearly knocking Albert Lee down as she ran away from the car and he ran toward it.

I had heard the screaming, but didn't see the near collision. Albert Lee told me about that later after he had gotten me out and slammed the door, trapping the snake inside, coiled now on the backseat. Probably more scared than we were, though I didn't think about that at the time. All I was thinking was that we were out and alive.

Now, gliding around the curves next to my

just-a-little-bit-snakebit sister and a paramedic who was going to be blind soon if she didn't cut her bangs, I tried to think who might have wanted to scare us away from Chandler Mountain and why. We had found Susan's body, we had looked through Monk Crawford's house, and I had met Betsy Mahall for lunch. We had also seen some of the handlers, had met a couple of them, Joe Baker in particular. We had gotten to know the Packards, mother and son, and had found out that Eugene Mahall was a tyrant, perhaps a murderer, and that he could walk. But he didn't know that we knew that. And even if he did, what would he be afraid of? That we might tell Betsy?

Whoever had put the snake in the car had done it in the short time that we had been drinking coffee with Betsy, returning the key. Albert Lee Packard's car had been the only one that had come up while we were there.

Someone hiding in the church? Parked on the other side of it? Or someone sneaking up through the woods? And who was afraid of what we might know? What *did* we know?

"Virgil will figure everything out," Sister said, reading my thoughts.

I sighed; it hurt.

"Hey. You back again?" Irene, the receptionist in the emergency room at the Blount County Medical Center, looked up in surprise.

I pointed to the ambulance where Mary Alice was being unloaded. "It's my sister this time. She's been bitten by a snake."

233

"Well, have mercy. Y'all are smack in the middle of some kind of bad karma, aren't you? Work in here long enough you see bad karma, Southern Baptist or not."

She handed me a clipboard with a form to fill out. "What kind of snake was it?"

"Rattlesnake."

"In January?

"Somebody put it in our car."

"Well, I declare. You sure?"

"It was sitting on the back seat big as life last time I saw it."

"Lord. I'd have died just seeing it."

"I almost did."

I squinted at the form, and reached in my purse for my reading glasses. Behind me the doors banged open as the gurney was brought in.

"Wait a minute," I called to Tammy as they started down the hall. "I've got to get her purse. I need the insurance cards." Lord, déjà vu sure enough. The feeling was compounded when I sat down to fill out the form and Death walked in with his KILL THEM ALL, LET GOD SORT THEM OUT T-shirt on, sat down, and picked up a *Southern Living*.

I glanced over at Irene.

"Trash," she mouthed.

The door slid open again with a rush of cold air.

"Mrs. Hollowell?"

I looked up to see Terry Mahall. He was dressed in a navy suit with a red-and-navy-striped tie. He was every inch the banker today.

"Betsy called and told me you were here. She wanted me to check and see how your sister is. Albert called her and told her what happened."

"They've just taken her back. I think she's going to be okay, though. I appreciate your coming by."

Terry sat down beside me. Death looked over the top of his *Southern Living*, checked him out, and continued his reading.

"I'm glad Betsy called me. I'm working right down the street today so if there's anything I can do for you, I'll be glad to."

"Thanks, but I can't think of a thing. Did she tell you what happened?"

"She sure did. Unbelievable."

Death's cute little wife walked in, and he stood up. For the first time, Terry got a look at the T-shirt.

"Lord," he mumbled. Then after they walked out, "I hope we're not financing anything for him."

I shrugged, which hurt. I may have groaned a little.

"Are you okay?" Terry asked.

"I think so."

"Your face is scratched pretty bad. And burned. The air bag?"

I nodded.

"Well, I think we need to get you checked out, too." He got up and started toward Irene, then turned back to me. "Okay?"

Polite man. I was happy for him to take charge.

"Okay."

Fifteen minutes later I was being wheeled down to X-ray. An hour later I was sharing a cubicle with Sister, my two cracked ribs were wrapped, the abrasions on my face were covered with antibiotic salve, and I was feeling no pain.

"What did they give you?" Sister asked. "You're pie-eyed."

"I don't know, but this is a nice place."

"Hell. They haven't done a thing for me. Keep looking in my eyes and making me pee in a bottle."

"Well, my goodness. I'll bet that's hard to do." I studied the vertical blue-and-gray lines in the wallpaper. Interesting.

"That Mahall guy said to tell you he had to go but he would check on you later."

"That's nice."

"And Virgil's on his way down here. He says Virginia called Richard to come get her."

"She and Luke should get married."

"Dear God. What did they give you?"

I didn't know and I didn't care. The blue and gray lines in the wallpaper were beautiful.

"My baby," Fred said. "My sweet baby." He ran his hand over my hair.

"Sister hit a mailbox," I said.

"I know she did." He took my hand and held it.

"It was a damn Godzilla of a rattlesnake." Sister started crying.

I opened my eyes. A nurse was taking my

blood pressure and Sister was sobbing into the shoulder of Virgil Stuckey's uniform.

"Where's Fred?" I asked.

The nurse took the cup off of my arm and pushed my hair back to examine the abrasions on my forehead.

"He'll be here in a little while," Virgil said. "I called him."

"You're fine." The nurse patted my arm. "Go back to sleep."

And I did.

"Wake up, honey. It's time to go home."

This time I knew I wasn't dreaming.

"Where's Sister?" I asked.

"Virgil's taking her home. They left when I got here. She's fine. How about you?"

I sat up very carefully. Surprisingly, there was little pain.

"I'm okay."

"You're drunk as a coot. They're going to wheel you out to the car."

"Sister hit a mailbox, Fred."

"That's what I heard." He grinned. "Mark that one off your list."

"I can't wait to tell Haley and Debbie."

"You little snitch."

"What goes around, comes around."

It sounded like it made sense.

It was the next afternoon before I got around to E-mailing Haley, though. And then I wasn't sure how much I should tell her. Her Aunt

Sister hitting the mailbox, definitely. But how much did I want to tell her about the snakes and the murders?

Debbie had called around ten o'clock to check on me. Her mother had told her about the snake and the car wreck, and that the snake was as big as a boa constrictor, and was I all right?

I told her that I was feeling pretty good, that Fred had brought me a couple of aspirin, coffee, and the morning paper before he left, and I was still in bed but considering getting up.

"Did your mama tell you she hit a mailbox?" I couldn't resist.

"You're kidding. No, I swear she told me a tree, Aunt Pat." Debbie giggled. "You gonna let her live it down?"

"I'm storing it away for future use. How's Brother?"

"He slept two straight hours last night. I guess that's progress. Have you heard from Haley?"

"I haven't turned on the computer since yesterday morning. I think they'll be back from Rome today." I hesitated. "I don't think I'll tell her about the snake and the wreck." I thought for a moment. "Well, about the wreck. I can't resist. But not why it happened. No use worrying her."

"I can't believe somebody put a big rattlesnake in Mama's car. And that it bit her."

"She lucked out with the gloves," I admitted.

"I trust the two of you are going to stay away from Chandler Mountain?"

"You trust right. Virgil Stuckey is welcome

to Chandler Mountain and all the goings-on up there. Incidentally, Debbie, I think I heard him call Sister, 'my baby.' You really may get yourself a stepfather out of this one."

"Lord have mercy, Aunt Pat. How does the woman do it?"

"Haley says it's pheromones and the woman ought to bottle them."

We hung up laughing. At least Debbie was laughing. My ribs were too painful. Go back to Chandler Mountain? No way. I took the phone off the hook, turned gingerly on my side, and went back to sleep with no thought of the old saying about the mountains coming to Mohammed. A good thing or I wouldn't have slept so soundly.

Chapter Nineteen

E-MAIL
FROM: HALEY
TO: MAMA AND PAPA
SUBJECT: ROME

The pope actually spoke to me, y'all. He said, "How do you do, Mrs. Nachman." Isn't that incredible? "How do you do, Mrs. Nachman." We've been married five months and I think it was the first time that I really felt like Mrs. Nachman, not like Haley Hollowell

Buchanan pretending to be Haley Nachman. And he held out his hand and I didn't think I was supposed to shake it so I held out my hand to let him take the initiative and he took it in both of his and just held it. And he asked where we were from and I told him Birmingham, Alabama, and he said he had heard it was a beautiful city and I said it is, that it's mountainous and green and he should come visit us. And then he asked if I wanted him to bless me and I said yes, and could he include my family. Which he did, so all of you are blessed.

He's not as frail as I thought he would be. And he has the most unforgettable eyes. They're like blue marbles. Philip says he thinks they're some kind of special contact lenses. Whatever. They're remarkable.

Then we visited the tourist sites. Even threw some coins in the Trevi Fountain because we want to go back some day. Telling you about that is going to wait until tomorrow, though. We've just gotten back and it's late and we're tired. A good, happy tired.

Love to everyone. Tell them all that they're blessed.

Haley

The back door slammed and Sister called, "Mouse?"

"In the boys' room with the computer."

I heard her stop by the refrigerator, heard ice clunking, and then the opening of a cabinet.

240

"We're all blessed," I told her when she came into the room eating chocolate chip cookies and drinking a Coke. I moved aside so she could read Haley's E-mail.

"Probably the reason Luke and Virginia and Richard left," she said when she finished reading.

"They've gone home?"

"Richard's gone back to Washington. Luke and Virginia have gone to Columbus."

"They were speaking?"

Sister got up from the computer and sat on one of the twin beds that have been in the room since Freddie and Alan were children. I've never been able to totally turn the room over to an office. And the beds come in handy sometimes.

"Sort of," she said.

"Sort of?"

"Virginia told Luke to go to hell, and he told her to kiss his butt."

"Well, at least they're communicating."

We smiled at each other.

Sister crammed a whole chocolate chip cookie in her mouth. held up her hand, chewed, swallowed, and said that they had to stay where Virgil could get in touch with them.

"He talked to them a long time last night, though," she added. "Luke admitted that maybe it wasn't Virginia who hit him over the head in the church, that it was more an impression of someone coming at him, and he'd just seen Susan's body and was rattled."

She took a long swallow of Coke. "And Virginia said it sure as hell wasn't her, that

241

she was in Nashville by then getting ready to Senior Swing." She held out the package of cookies. "Want some?"

I shook my head. "Are you feeling okay?"

"Fine. I had a little headache when I woke up and then Virginia told me they were leaving. I didn't even have to take an aspirin. How about you? You look like hell."

"I don't feel as bad as I look. How did you get over here?"

"The Jag folks gave me a demonstrator to drive while mine's in the shop. Nice. I may upgrade."

Those Jag folks aren't fools.

"Does Virgil have any idea what's going on up on Chandler Mountain?"

"I don't think he's supposed to talk about it."

Which probably meant he didn't have a clue.

Sister downed another cookie, chugalugged the rest of the Coke, and announced that she was on her way to the Big, Bold, and Beautiful Shoppe for some loungewear, that Virgil was coming over for supper, and she figured something in velour would be nice. What did I think? And did I want to go with her? Bonnie Blue would pee her pants when she heard about the rattlesnake.

I doubted that, but Bonnie Blue Butler is one of the shrewdest women I've ever known. I thought it would be interesting to run the whole story by her. And I hadn't seen her since before we went to Warsaw. She hadn't heard about our trip.

"Don't worry about the way you look," Sister said. "If anybody notices, they'll just think you've been in a bad fire and haven't had skin grafts yet."

"Do, Jesus," Bonnie Blue exclaimed when she looked up from the package she was wrapping and saw me. "Did the Concorde fall down?"

"Mary Alice hit a mailbox yesterday."

When I saw the expression on Bonnie Blue's face, I decided right then and there that the pain was going to be worth it.

"No," she said to Sister. "You hit a mailbox and skinned this girl up like this?"

"Only because a rattlesnake was hanging on to me." Sister held out her hand, which was still swollen and discolored.

Bonnie Blue frowned.

"If I'm lying, I'm dying," Sister assured her.

"Well, I've got to hear about this." Bonnie Blue reached into a bin, pulled out a pink bow, and stuck it on the package. She held it up for our inspection and we nodded that it was fine.

We followed her to the comfortable seating arrangement in the front corner of the store. Since Bonnie Blue has been the manager of the Big, Bold, and Beautiful Shoppe, she has made her mark on the store, the "getting your thoughts together area" as she calls it being one of them. Sister and I sat on the flowered chintz loveseat and Bonnie Blue offered us coffee, which we both declined before she sat in the matching chair and said, "Now, what's this about a rattlesnake?"

Bonnie Blue looked wonderful, I realized. She is as large as Sister with skin the color of dark milk chocolate. The two of them walking down the street together is a formidable sight. But today Bonnie Blue was dressed in a soft pink suit and her hair was pulled back from her forehead and held with a pink hairband.

"You look like you had a great Christmas," I said.

She cut her eyes around at me and grinned. "Girlfriend, you wouldn't believe. But y'all tell me your stuff first."

Mary Alice did most of the talking. Did a pretty good job of it, too, only wandering off the subject occasionally to describe the Mahall house and its Thomas Jefferson floors and Albert Packard's Spanish-moss beard.

Bonnie Blue is one of the best listeners in the world, nodding, breaking in to say a friend of her daddy's had been killed in the Daisy Belle mine explosion and didn't we remember it?

"Seems like I remember something about it," Sister said.

"Some of those men are still buried up there in that coal mine. Mr. R. T. Jemison, Daddy's friend, is one of them."

"Did the company pay his wife much?" I asked.

"Don't know. I can find out."

"I don't guess it matters. It's just that that's supposed to be how the Mahall man got his money."

"Wouldn't surprise me," Bonnie Blue said.

"That accident made them change a bunch of the laws."

"This lady on the mountain told us that everybody believes Eugene Mahall killed his second wife, a country singer named Louellen Conway," I added.

Bonnie Blue'e eyes rounded. "Kicking Balls?"

Mary Alice and I both must have looked confused.

"You know the song, 'Kicking Balls.' That was Louellen Conway's claim to fame."

Bonnie Blue waited for a sign of recognition, which she failed to get.

"You know. It's supposed to be about a football game or a soccer game, but that's not really what it's about. It's a woman's song. A friend of mine gave it to me. First time I played it I was driving down 459 and got to laughing so hard I had to pull over." Bonnie Blue giggled in remembrance. "Y'all need to hear that song. They didn't play it much on the radio. Men disc jockeys. I'll see if I can get you a copy."

"I wonder if she made the record after she married Eugene Mahall," I said. "Maybe that's the reason she's supposed to be part of the interstate ramp."

"Louellen Conway? Hell, y'all, if we're talking about the same person, she's right here in Birmingham. One of my best customers."

"Must not be the same person then." Sister turned to me. "Didn't Miss Beulah say Louellen was little and blond?"

I nodded.

"Well, this Louellen's blond, but she's a size twenty-four. How long's it been since all this happened?"

"Several years."

Bonnie Blue got up. "Tell you what. Why don't I call her and ask her if she was ever married to what's his name again?"

"Eugene Mahall."

Sister got up, too. "While you're doing that, I'm going to be looking around. Something for an at-home evening. Maybe purple velour."

Bonnie Blue pointed toward the left side of the shop and Sister headed in that direction. I picked up a *People* and tried to get interested in what the actresses had worn to Christmas parties. But my mind was too busy. If this Louellen Conway was the one who had been married to Eugene Mahall, chances were that she knew Monk Crawford, Susan, Joe Baker, and the rest of the handlers. Or at least knew about them. She certainly could tell us about Eugene Mahall, who was looming as a more sinister character all the time. Had she known he could walk? Had he always taken advantage of his son Terry? I thought about Betsy and the two children caught in that situation.

"Louellen?" I heard Bonnie Blue say. "It's Bonnie Blue."

A pause.

"Sure. I stuck it back for you. The one with the bird on it, too."

Pause.

"Just whenever. No problem. But, listen,

Louellen. Were you ever married to a man by the name of Eugene Mahall?"

I looked up. Bonnie Blue was holding her hand over the phone and grinning. "Y'all hit a nerve," she told Sister and me. She put the phone back to her ear and said, "Uh huh" several times. There were also a "Have mercy" and "You don't say." Then, "A couple of ladies. One of them got snakebit up on Chandler Mountain yesterday. She's okay. She's in here now. But they heard this Mahall guy killed you and poured you into cement on an interstate ramp. I told them no way, that you were right here, alive and kicking."

There was another prolonged period of listening. Sister located two velour outfits, which she pulled out and hung on a hook. One was lavender, the other black. I knew which one she would leave the shop with. She disappeared into the dressing room.

"I'll tell them," Bonnie Blue said. "Sure. Tomorrow will be fine."

She hung up, jotted something down on a notepad, tore it out, and brought it to me.

"It's her phone number. She was married to him, all right. Says she'll tell you anything you want to know about the man, but none of it will be good, believe me. She was bad-mouthing that man something fierce."

"Thanks, Bonnie Blue." I stuck the phone number into the side of my purse. I wasn't sure I wanted to hear a tirade about Eugene Mahall. But if she might know anything about the snake handlers on Chandler Mountain, I'd like to hear that. I'd give her a call, find

247

out if she thought Betsy had any reason to be scared in that house.

"How about this?"

Sister was standing before us in the lavender velour suit.

"You look like an iris," Bonnie Blue said, clasping her hands together in joy. An iris? The woman had risen to manager of the shop within six months of starting work there. Easy to see why.

"You've got you a new man, Mary Alice. I can tell."

Sister nodded. I swear, blushing a little.

"He's the sheriff of St. Clair County," I said. "Named Virgil Stuckey. Calls her Baby."

"Well, I declare. Tell me all about him."

Which Sister did, transforming him into something Michelangelo might have sculpted. Then Bonnie Blue told us about Charlie, the man she had met over Christmas, and we heard that he was also straight from the sculptor's chisel.

"Haley met the pope," I said while Bonnie Blue paused for breath.

But the pope couldn't hold a candle to Virgil and Charlie. If another customer hadn't come in, and Bonnie Blue's assistant been out with the flu, we'd still be there.

I considered taking Woofer for a walk when I got home, but clouds were building in from the west, and the sharp wind that had sprung up was stinging my face. My ribs weren't as sore as I had thought they would be, but walking on the concrete sidewalks might jar them, make them hurt. I settled for giving Woofer a treat, went back into the den, and collapsed on the sofa. Muffin jumped up beside me, and she and I were both sound asleep when the doorbell rang. It rang a second time before I realized it wasn't part of my dream. It rang a third time before I got to the door.

I looked through the peephole and saw Spanish moss. Albert Lee Packard.

"God, you look awful," he said when I opened the door.

"Thanks. And aren't you tactful."

He grinned. "Sorry. How are you feeling?"

"Not as bad as I look."

"Good."

I gave him my schoolteacher look which he recognized. He laughed and held out a Piggly Wiggly sack that was folded several times at the top and that he was holding with his hand under the bottom.

"I'm on my way to Tuscaloosa and Mama wanted me to stop by and check on you and bring you this soup. She said you probably wouldn't be up to snuff today."

"I can't believe you said that."

He laughed again. "I've been waiting an hour to say that. I thought you'd appreciate it."

"I appreciate the soup."

"There's a pone of cornbread in there, too."

"Your mama is an angel. You want some coffee?"

"Sure. And I'd like to borrow your bathroom."

"Down the hall," I pointed. "Then come on back to the kitchen."

I was plugging in the percolator when he came in and sat down at the kitchen table.

"Nice house," he said. "Homey."

"Thanks. We like it. We had the bay window put in several years ago, the skylights in the den, too."

I got out a plate for the few chocolate chip cookies that remained in the package after Mary Alice's feeding frenzy and put them on the table.

"Did you know that Louellen Mahall isn't dead?" I asked him.

"Balls?" he grinned. "Sure. She was living here in Birmingham last I heard."

"Well, what was that wild story about the interstate ramp then? Where did that come from?"

"God knows. It's like the Chandler Mountain booger. It's been told so much that everybody believes it. I think my mother could run into Louellen on the street, have a conversation with her, and still believe she's cemented in the highway." He stroked his beard. "Stories like that fascinate me, don't they you? The way they become truth."

"To a certain point. Until they start hurting people. Everybody thinking he'd killed his wife must have bothered Eugene Mahall."

"I doubt it. More incentive for people to pay their bank loans on time."

I looked up, surprised at the sudden bitterness in his voice. "I take it that he's not exactly Mr. Popularity in St. Clair County."

"You're right about that. And this goes back a long way. Everybody still believes he knew more about the Daisy Belle mine explosion than he ever admitted. That there could have been some criminal indictments, but he lined his pockets instead."

"This isn't an interstate-ramp story?"

"I don't think so."

The coffee quit perking. I got up, poured us each a cup, and sat back down.

"Tell me about Terry and Betsy," I said, passing the sugar. "We were surprised when we found out they were living with him."

"He probably insists on it. I think they ask old man Mahall's permission to breathe. Terry tried sowing a few wild oats when he was a teenager, nothing much, and he got slapped in a military academy. And I think Betsy's so crazy about Terry that she'll put up with anything." Albert put two teaspoons of sugar in his coffee and stirred.

"Betsy says he's fond of the children, that he rides them around on his wheelchair."

Albert shrugged and sipped his coffee, holding his beard back.

"She says Terry's thrilled to have them, too, which is good."

"Not surprising. They're Susan's children." Albert dabbed at his beard with a napkin and then reached for a cookie.

I'm sure I looked startled.

He stopped with the cookie halfway to his mouth. "What? Terry was crazy about Susan when they were teenagers. You didn't know? That was when he got into some trouble,

251

when she married Ethan Crawford. I remember one thing he did was break all of the windows out of Monk's church."

"That was a long time ago."

Albert nodded. "But last year he asked Betsy for a divorce. After Ethan was killed."

"He did? Because of Susan?"

"According to the Chandler Mountain grapevine." He bit into the cookie, chewed, and took another sip of coffee while my mind was racing.

"No. It was more than the grapevine," Albert Lee added. "Betsy told my mother. Mama said she cried like a baby, said she was going to get Terry to counseling."

"They looked a lot alike, didn't they? Betsy and Susan."

"Which everybody was reminded of when Terry married Betsy."

I picked up my coffee and drank some of it. All kinds of thoughts were racing through my mind. Terry had asked Betsy for a divorce because he was in love with Susan. Betsy couldn't have children. Now she had two, and Susan was dead. "I'm scared," she had said. She had been worried about where the cameo was. Susan's body had been laid out neatly on the church bench. Luke had thought it was Virginia behind him. It could have been another woman.

Oh, surely not.

"Who do you think killed Susan and Monk?" I asked Albert.

"The Chandler Mountain booger."

As soon as Albert left, I raced to the phone

and called Mary Alice. For once I didn't get her answering machine.

"What are you doing?" I asked. "You won't believe what I've got to tell you."

"Taking a bubble bath. Some of that freesia stuff Debbie and Henry gave me for Christmas. It smells wonderful."

"And you're talking on the phone? You're going to get electrocuted, fool."

"Don't be silly, Mouse. It's the cell phone anyway. What's up?"

I told her about Albert Lee Packard's visit, about Terry Mahall being in love with Susan Crawford and asking Betsy for a divorce. I told her the whole story and ended with, "I think Betsy may have killed her sister."

"Wait a minute," Sister said. I heard water running into the tub. "It was getting cold," she explained when she picked up the phone again.

"Well, what do you think?" I asked.

"I think not."

"And why not?" I could envision a whole bathtub full of bubbles and Mary Alice.

"How could she have carried her into the church? Betsy's a little woman."

"So was Susan, and the adrenaline was pouring. People pick up pianos when the adrenaline's pouring."

"Well, how could she have put the rattlesnake in my car? She was right there with us the whole time. Somebody else had to sneak up and do that."

Damn. She was right.

"I'll figure it out," I said. "Enjoy your bath."

"You should take one, too, and relax. I know you don't have any bubble bath, but that Palmolive liquid that you bathe Woofer with for fleas ought to work."

I hung up.

E-MAIL
FROM: **MAMA AND PAPA**
TO: **HALEY**
SUBJECT: HAPPY ABOUT THE POPE

Honey, I'm so delighted that you had a wonderful trip to Rome and actually got to shake the pope's hand. We're all fine. No news. Love to both of you.
  Mama

Well, I certainly couldn't tell her about her Aunt Sister being bitten by a rattlesnake and us having a wreck. Especially after she'd just had us blessed.

Chapter Twenty

The soup was delicious. We topped it off with some pralines and cream ice cream that had been in the freezer so long it was chewy around the edges. But still good. Afterward, while I was leaning over putting the dishes in the dishwasher, Fred enveloped me in a bear hug and said, "You interested?"

"No."

"Me neither. I just wanted you to know the potential is still there."

"Good. How about you and the potential going and turning on *Biography*. I'll be there in a minute."

A half-hour later, Fred, the potential, and I were all sound asleep halfway through Nelson Rockefeller's life. Nelson was dead and buried and they were showing American castles when the phone rang for so long, I couldn't ignore it. I was lying on the sofa and I reached behind me and knocked the whole phone off the end table.

Muffin went skittering into the kitchen, and Fred opened one eye then closed it.

Damn. Damn. I got down on my hands and knees and found the receiver under the table. This had better not be one of those call-every-night-at-suppertime charities.

I thought whoever it was might have hung up, but when I answered, a woman said, "Mrs. Hollowell?"

"Yes." I waited to hear that their truck would be in our neighborhood next week picking up discards, but the woman surprised me.

"This is Louellen Conway. Bonnie Blue Butler said you were asking about me today. Are you all right? Would you rather that I call back some other time?"

"Oh, no. This is fine. I just knocked the phone off the table. We got back from Europe a few days ago and I'm still a little jet-lagged."

A slight tinkly laugh. "I know how that is. They say it's a day for every decade of your age."

I glanced over at Fred whose mouth was open. "At least."

"Well, Bonnie Blue told me about your wreck and the snakebite. She said you wanted to know about Eugene."

"We heard he killed you."

"Almost. It's taken a lot of Prozac and a lot of years to get over that episode in my life."

"Well, do you mind telling me what happened? There are two little children living in that house now that I'm frightened for."

"Susan's children. I read about it in the paper. Why are you frightened for them?"

"Because I think there's a distinct possibility that either Terry or Betsy might have killed their mother."

"Oh, I doubt that seriously. Why do you think so?"

I glanced over at Fred who seemed to be sound asleep. His mouth was still open. But I decided to take no chances. He hates for me to get tangled up in anything more dangerous than meeting with the investment club that Sister and I belong to. Which, come to think of it, can be pretty dangerous at times. Anyway, I don't like to worry him.

"Let me go in the bedroom and take this," I said.

Sitting on the bed, I told her the whole story,

including Albert Lee Packard's visit and the news that Terry had been planning on leaving Betsy for Susan. I also included the fact that it was believed on Chandler Mountain that Eugene Mahall had feathered his nest with the mining company's money.

I finished with, "And did you know he can walk?"

"A few steps. He'd do a lot better if he'd stuck to his physical therapy."

Louellen cleared her throat. "Now let me tell you what I know."

"Okay."

"Let me light a cigarette."

There was a pause. Then, "Eugene Mahall adored his wife. He adored his son, and I'm sure he did feather his nest. God only knows why he married me or why I married him. He's mean as a snake, and I was a drunk. I'd been hanging around Nashville for years, had one hit, 'Kicking Balls,' and couldn't handle it. I was broke and singing at a club called the Tennessee Line. Eugene came in several nights and then one night he asked me to marry him. And I thought, 'Well, hell, why not? I'll straighten myself up and be a good wife for this poor rich man in a wheelchair. That shouldn't be hard to do.' Hah. Shows how clear I was thinking."

"Did he physically abuse you?"

"No. He didn't touch me. Turned out what he wanted from me was children. Lots of them. I guess he thought he was going to start a Mahall dynasty. God knows why he picked me. And I'd failed to tell him about my little hysterectomy. Just didn't think it was important. When he found out, he totally ignored me. And I needed help, honey, let me tell you."

"What about Terry?"

"If I could have had children, I wouldn't. Not after I saw the way Eugene treated Terry. I don't think the child's ever had a thought of his own."

I doubted that last statement. I asked Louellen if she had known any of the snake handlers.

"I knew Monk Crawford. And Susan, of course. I know Eugene had a fit when he found out that Terry's girlfriend was one of that crowd. Told him he couldn't date her."

"Well, do you think he'll welcome her children?"

"He'll conveniently forget their background, turn them into Mahall clones."

There was silence for a moment. I could imagine Louellen taking long drags from her cigarette, the smoke curling toward the ceiling.

"How did you get out?" I asked. I had no idea if she would answer or not, but it seemed important to know.

"Monk Crawford came to paint the house one day. When he left, I went with him."

That sounded so familiar I almost laughed. For a moment I wondered how things were going in Columbus with Luke and Virginia.

"But, Mrs. Hollowell," she continued, "I truly don't think you have to worry about those children's safety. Children are what Eugene's always wanted."

And what Terry and Betsy hadn't been able to give him.

I thanked her for her help and hung up with the promise to let her know if I learned anything about the murders. Then I stepped into a warm shower, closed my eyes, and tried to relax. Terry Mahall had handed over to his father what he had always wanted, the beginning of a dynasty. Or had it been Betsy? One more reason for Susan Crawford's death.

The next morning was cold, but clear. I warmed the leftover soup from the night before and put it into a thermos for Fred's lunch, kissed him goodbye, and went to check my E-mail. Nothing. Even the large lesbians seemed to have deserted me. I got Woofer's leash, and we walked around several blocks. My face still looked as if I had been in a fight, but it felt better.

As we came back by Mitzi's house, she opened the front door and called, "How's Brother?"

"Fine. I'm going over there this morning. You want to go?"

"Can't. I've got to keep Andrew Cade while Bridget goes shopping. Tell Debbie I'll be over soon, though."

I wanted grandchildren close enough to keep while their mothers went shopping. Lisa and Alan and our two grandsons have always lived in Atlanta, a little too far for a drop-in visit. Haley, get pregnant with twins, I said to the morning sky. A boy and a girl. I'll baby-sit all you want.

I gave Mitzi a wave and opened the gate. A couple of treats for Woofer, which he took into his igloo, and I was in the kitchen pouring myself my second cup of coffee. Morning sun was gleaming across the white table in the bay window. Muffin was lying across the heating vent and cat hairs were flying. Probably worse than Mary Alice's Bubba Cat on his heating pad on the kitchen counter. I moved Muffin over to her rug. She immediately got up and moved back to the vent. How was I going to bear parting with her when Haley came back?

It was an ordinary day. I sat at the table and glanced through the paper. Bosnia, Kosovo. The statue of Vulcan was falling apart. The crack in his butt had widened some more; he would have to be taken down to be repaired. I tried to imagine Red Mountain without Vulcan's bare rear end mooning us every-time we drove anywhere on the south side of the mountain. They couldn't take him down. Surely there was some other solution.

It was still an ordinary day when Sister came in the back door and said she was going over to Debbie's and did I want to go.

I did.

Well, let her run to the bathroom a minute. She had so much to tell me about last night, I wouldn't believe.

The first inkling that it was not an ordinary day was when she came back into the kitchen holding up a brown leather wallet.

"Whose is this? It was on the floor in the bathroom."

"Don't know. Look inside and see. You want some coffee?"

"Okay." She handed me the wallet. "You look. I'll get the coffee."

And then I remembered. "I'll bet it's Albert Lee Packard's. He used the hall bathroom when he came by here to bring the soup." I opened it and saw the picture on his driver's license. His beard hung below the camera's head shot, so it was impossible to see how long it was.

"That's one more ugly beard," Sister said, looking over my shoulder. "How old is he, anyway?"

I looked at the date on the license. "Forty-six."

"He ought to do better than that. Makes him look like a troll. Billygoat Gruff." Sister sat down and reached for the sugar. "What else is in there?"

"None of our business."

"Well, of course it is." She put down the sugar and took the wallet from me. "It was on your bathroom floor."

Sometimes Sister's reasoning defies reason.

"Let's see. Forty-eight dollars. A Visa and a library card. Blue Cross. And a whole pack of pictures."

"Put that up," I said. "I'll call his mother and tell her it's here. I'll bet he's worried to death about it."

"Hmm. Mouse, all of these pictures are of the dead girl."

Maybe that was the moment that the day really ceased being ordinary.

"What? Susan Crawford?" I reached over and grabbed the insert of pictures. Sister was right. There was Susan Crawford in a bathing suit, Susan Crawford pregnant, her hands folded on her large belly, Susan Crawford in a glamour pose, one made in a studio, her red hair pulled over her shoulder provocatively. I pulled it from its plastic cover and looked at it closely. What a beautiful girl she had been. Betsy was pretty, but Susan had been a knockout.

"There's something written on the back," Sister said.

I turned it over. In a childish half-cursive, half-printed handwriting was the inscription, "To my Chandler Mountain booger. With love, Susan."

"Who do you think killed Susan, Albert?"

"The Chandler Mountain booger."

The words were as clear as if Albert Lee were in the kitchen. I handed the picture to Mary Alice and pressed my shaking hands together.

"What's the matter?" she asked. "You sick?"

"I know who killed Susan Crawford."

"Who?"

I nodded toward the picture she was holding. "The Chandler Mountain booger. Albert Lee Packard."

She looked at the inscription on the back of the picture. "What makes you say that? This booger thing is just a joke."

"This part isn't." I told her what Albert Lee had said the night before.

"I don't believe that for one minute. I know for a fact that Virgil thinks Joe Baker killed

Susan and Monk. And why would Albert Lee have done it anyway?"

"He was in love with her, had been for years."

"So?"

"When Ethan died, maybe Albert Lee thought it was finally his chance, and she turned him down."

"That's dumb. I've turned lots of men down and they haven't killed me."

I closed my eyes and thought. I knew I was right, but I was having trouble putting two and two together here.

"He was the only person we know who was out there when the snake was put in your car, remember?"

"But he's not a snake handler."

"Doesn't matter. He could have gotten a snake anywhere on that mountain."

I picked up the wallet and looked in it again. Behind the money was a cash receipt from Rich's, $2,472.92, FINE JEWELRY. It was dated December 23. I handed it to Sister.

"Engagement ring?"

She shrugged. "Could have been anything."

"Not on a teacher's salary. Especially a book collector."

The doorbell rang. I caught my breath.

"It's Albert Lee. I know it is." And I did know it, just as sure as I knew he had killed Susan Crawford.

"Here." I handed her the wallet. "Put the pictures back in and throw it in the bathroom, quick."

"Hell. Last night you figured out it was Terry

263

and Betsy." But she pushed her chair back while she was inserting the pack of pictures. "Take your time so I can get back in the kitchen. It's probably not him, anyway."

But my intuition was right. I got the same view of the scraggly beard through the peephole that I had gotten the day before.

"Okay," Sister called. By this time the doorbell had rung twice.

I opened the door. "Good morning, Albert Lee. Sorry. I was on the phone."

"Morning, Mrs. Hollowell. I'm sorry to bother you, but I was wondering if by any chance you've seen my billfold."

"Why, no, Albert Lee." God, what an awful actor I am. I should have just handed the damn thing to him and hoped he would believe we hadn't looked in it.

"Well, do you mind if I look in your bathroom? I was thinking it might have slipped out in there."

"You're welcome to look. I hope it's there. I lost my billfold at Sears several years ago and I was in a panic, but some nice lady found it and turned it in to Lost and Found. Everything was there, credit cards and all. I thought for sure I was going to have to call and cancel them."

He stood there looking at me. Oh, God. He knew I knew. It was the babbling.

"May I come in?"

"Of course."

"I can't get by you."

"Oh, pardon." I moved aside.

"Is something wrong?"

"I just had some bad news." I hoped to

264

hell he didn't ask me what. I was too rattled to come up with something sensible.

"I'm sorry. Well, I won't be but a minute."

I watched him turn and go down the hall. Maybe I was wrong. He was an English teacher, for God's sake. English teachers didn't go around murdering people. Even English teachers who looked like Rip van Winkle. Sister was right. The Chandler Mountain booger was a joke.

"Here it is," he said, coming back holding up the wallet. "Thank goodness."

"Thank goodness," I echoed. I was still reminding myself that he was an English teacher not a murderer as he said goodbye and stepped onto the porch. But just as I was about to close the door, he turned and asked if he could get the Tupperware bowl that he had brought the soup in. He had promised his mother he would bring it back.

"Of course. I should have thought of it. I'll get it for you."

"And could I bother you for some water? I took some aspirin a while ago for a headache and they're stuck about halfway down."

An English teacher. Not a murderer.

"Come on back to the kitchen. You want a Coke?"

Sister was sitting at the kitchen table reading the paper.

"Morning, Albert Lee," she said. "What brings you out this early?"

"Morning, Mrs. Crane. I dropped my wallet in Mrs. Hollowell's hall bathroom yesterday afternoon."

"Well, I declare. I'm glad you found it."

"So am I."

"Sit down," Sister said, pushing a chair back with her foot. "How's your mama?"

"Fine." Then, "Just water, Mrs. Hollowell. Thanks.

"I've got an aspirin stuck halfway down," he explained to Sister.

"I hate when that happens. You need to get the coated kind."

Four things happened then almost simultaneously. I put the Tupperware bowl and a glass of water in front of Albert Lee, Sister folded the newspaper, the receipt from Rich's Fine Jewelry drifted from the table, and Albert Lee reached down and picked it up saying, "You dropped something."

What happened next I'll always blame on Sister. If she hadn't said, "Oh, my God," and grabbed for the receipt, chances were that Albert Lee wouldn't have paid any attention to it.

But he did. When Sister's swipe at it missed, he looked to see what he was holding.

For a moment, I don't think any of the three of us breathed. Then Albert Lee stuck the receipt in his jacket pocket and drank the glass of water I had given him. Drank it slowly, looking out of the bay window.

"I like this house," he said. "I see your sasanquas are already blooming."

Sister and I glanced at each other. Maybe everything was okay. So he knew we had looked through his wallet. So what?

But everything was not okay.

"You know, don't you?" Albert Lee said almost dreamily.

"Know what?" Sister and I said together.

Albert Lee stood up, reached in his back pocket, and pulled out a small pistol.

"Come on, ladies. I guess we'll have to go see Mama."

Chapter Twenty-One

"Damn, damn, damn," Sister said in my ear while I was wrapping the tape around her ankles. "This is all your fault." She was sitting in the backseat of Albert Lee's car. Stuffed in, really. Albert's Neon had not been designed with Sister in mind.

"Shut up." I had already taped her wrists together with the clear reinforced tape that I was sure Albert Lee used when he shipped books. It had been in the glove compartment of his car and, surely, he didn't go around taping women up all the time.

"We're going to be all right," I whispered to Sister. "The man's an English teacher."

She banged her chin into the back of my head. It hurt like hell. I'd never before realized how pointed her chin was.

"Ow," I flinched back and felt a tiny circle of steel between my shoulders.

"Something wrong?" Albert Lee asked.

"She hurt me," I said, rubbing my head.

"Well, shame on you, big sister. Don't try that on me." He reached over with a penknife in his left hand, cut the tape, and pressed it down against Sister's ankle. Then he motioned with the pistol for me to get into the front seat, which I did and he taped my wrists and ankles. So much for our "Neighborhood Watch" program. Here we were being kidnapped in broad daylight at gunpoint and what everybody was watching was *The Price is Right* or *All My Children*.

"Albert Lee, why are you doing this?" Sister asked. "You're just going to get yourself into more trouble."

"Not if you just disappear off the face of the earth." He got in the car and pulled away from the curb.

"What is it you think we know anyway? We don't know a damn thing except you're kidnapping us," Sister said.

"You know I killed Susan."

"I don't know you killed Susan. Do you know he killed Susan, Patricia Anne?"

"I don't know it."

"Of course you do. You'd been through my wallet. You saw all the pictures, the receipt."

"You're jumping to conclusions, Albert Lee," I said.

"And so did you. The right one." He had turned right onto Valley Avenue by this time.

"Let us out," I said. The danger of the situation was just registering with me. We were being kidnapped by a murderer with a gun who was going to make us disappear off the face of the earth. "Let us out, Albert Lee. I don't know what happened to Susan, but kidnapping us is just going to compound your troubles."

"Shut up. Just shut up. I need to talk to Mama."

"The crack in Vulcan's butt is really getting wider, Patricia Anne. Look," Sister said, apropos of nothing. "He could fall right down here on Valley Avenue."

I wasn't interested in sightseeing or Vulcan's plight. I was trying to see if I could get my ankles loose. If I could, I could kick Albert Lee's leg, make him wreck. But we were going down steep and busy Twentieth Street now. If he swerved, it would be a terrible wreck. Chances were that we would hit another car head-on, a car full of innocent people.

"Why are you turning on First Avenue, Albert Lee?" Sister asked when he turned on his right signal. "Aren't we going to Chandler Mountain?"

"Goddamn interstates."

I looked over at Albert Lee. He didn't look good. He was pale and sweat was beaded on his forehead.

"Let us out, Albert Lee," I pleaded. "You're not a murderer. You're an English teacher."

"And you're crazy."

We crossed the viaduct over the Sloss Furnace Museum.

"Remember the big outdoor ad that used to be here for years?" Sister asked. "The one for dog food where the cute little puppy's tongue wagged? It always smelled like ham here. I guess it was the dog food plant."

I swear my sister never fails to amaze me. Here we were, kidnapped, on the verge of extinction, and she was carrying on a casual conversation about dog food.

"Penny dog food," Albert Lee said. He wiped his forehead with his right arm leaving a wet spot on the sleeve of his denim jacket. The butt of the pistol was clearly visible in the shallow jacket pocket.

"That's right," Sister said. "Penny. I couldn't remember which brand it was. Do you suppose it cost a penny when it first came out?"

Neither Albert Lee nor I answered.

We rode in silence for a few minutes. Then Sister said, "Oh, you're going up Highway 11. One of my husbands used to own some property up here. I should have held on to it. It's probably worth a fortune now. You know, sometimes I wish I'd buried them up here at Jefferson Memorial Gardens. Look how nice it looks without tombstones."

I swear you'd think we were going for a casual drive in the country.

"Albert Lee," I said. "I think I know why you killed Susan, but will you tell me why you killed Monk Crawford?"

He looked startled. "I didn't kill Monk. Hell, that brother-in-law of his did him in. Hated him."

"Because of the snakes?"

"Because Monk was giving the snakes up. You don't do that, not on Chandler Mountain. Not without paying for it." He wiped his forehead again. "Especially if you'd been the leader."

"Could Susan have left the group?"

"Probably. They're not so rigid with the women. They don't think they're important." He sighed. "But she didn't want to."

"Is that why you killed her? Because she wouldn't give up the snake handling?" I asked.

"Not that it's a damn bit of your business, but I loved her. I wanted to marry her and she laughed. It was simple as that. Then I took her to Mama."

"And you put her in the church."

"It was where she would have wanted to be. I couldn't do anything else for her." Tears were coursing down his face now. "I'd always loved her. I always will."

"Oh, look," Sister said. "We're in Trussville. I love the barbecue place here, don't you, Albert Lee?"

Albert Lee turned around. "Shut up."

There was another silence of about fifteen minutes before I brought up the subject of Susan Crawford again.

"Albert Lee, you were in the church, weren't you, when our cousin went in."

He nodded. "Brushing Susan's hair. Did you see that hair? A Rossetti painting."

"What did you do?"

"Ducked behind a pew. Mama saw him coming in. She hit him so I could get out."

And now we were going to die because

271

Luke had walked into a church. Pukey Lukey was going to be the death of us.

"You're going to get on the interstate in Springville, aren't you?" Sister asked.

Hadn't she been paying any attention to what we were talking about? I was trying to figure out some kind of strategy here and she was doing a travelogue. The woman was nuts.

"Guess I'll have to," Albert Lee said, wiping his face again. In spite of being scared to death, I felt sorry for him. Chances were that he had never known the violence existed in him that had welled up when Susan laughed at his proposal.

We turned off Highway 11 in Springville and headed for the interstate.

"Goddamn interstates. I hate them," Albert Lee said turning onto the entrance ramp. Below us the pond I had admired several days before shimmered in the sun. The black and white cows grazed in the pasture.

And below us, several police cars blocked the entrance.

"Shit," Albert Lee said, slamming on his brakes and throwing the car into reverse. But more police cars had pulled in behind us, lights flashing, sirens wailing.

Men in uniforms surrounded us, guns drawn.

"Oh, shit," Albert Lee said, clasping his arms around the steering wheel and laying his head on them.

"You did what?"

"She led us all the way," Virgil Stuckey said. "Isn't she something?"

We had just been untaped and were watching Albert Lee being led to a patrol car. Virgil had his arm around Sister and was looking at her as if she had just invented the wheel.

"I dialed 911 on my cell phone while Albert Lee was getting in the car," she said. "Everytime I mentioned a place, I was telling them where we were going."

"Well, I'll be damned," I said. "I'm proud of you."

Sister gave an aw-shucks shrug. "I saw a woman on CNN who had done it in Atlanta when she was carjacked," she admitted. "And my purse was on the floor right in front of me and I remembered it."

"She probably saved your life, you know," Virgil said. And I knew I would hear about it for the rest of my life.

I watched a handcuffed Albert Lee being put into the back of a patrol car. I couldn't believe it.

And him an English teacher.

"I heard," the phone message from Debbie said. "And I'm signing you both up for karate lessons. God knows you need them. And, Aunt Pat, if you haven't read your E-mail yet turn it on and then call me."

E-MAIL
FROM: **HALEY**
TO: **MAMA AND PAPA**

I'm E-mailing Debbie and telling her to save the neutercal. I'm going to need it Labor Day. Labor Day. Isn't that a nice coincidence? I was suspicious when you were here for Christmas but not positive. We're both so happy. No more unruffled retirement for you, Mama!
   I love you both so much,
    Haley

   I had just turned off the computer and was sniffling for joy when the phone rang.
   "Now aren't you glad I saved your life?" Sister asked.
   Told you.